R.2(

*Indulge in some perfect romance
from the incomparable*

PENNY JORDAN

**The all new Penny Jordan
large print collection gives you
your favourite glamorous
Penny Jordan stories in
easier-to-read print.**

Penny Jordan has been writing for more than twenty-five years and has an outstanding record: over 165 novels published including the phenomenally successful A PERFECT FAMILY, TO LOVE, HONOUR AND BETRAY, THE PERFECT SINNER and POWER PLAY which hit *The Sunday Times* and *New York Times* bestseller lists. She says she hopes to go on writing until she has passed the 200 mark, and maybe even the 250 mark.

Penny is a member and supporter of both the Romantic Novelists' Association and the Romance Writers of America—two organisations dedicated to providing support for both published and yet-to-be published authors.

PAST PASSION

Penny Jordan

First published in Great Britain 1991
Large Print Edition 2010
Harlequin Mills & Boon Limited,
Eton House, 18-24 Paradise Road,
Richmond, Surrey TW9 1SR

AudioGO

16·11·10

© Penny Jordan 1991

ISBN: 978 0 263 21684 4

Harlequin Mills & Boon policy is to use papers that are natural, renewable and recyclable products and made from wood grown in sustainable forests. The logging and manufacturing process conform to the legal environmental regulations of the country of origin.

Printed and bound in Great Britain
by CPI Antony Rowe, Chippenham, Wiltshire

CHAPTER ONE

As NICOLA climbed out of her small car, she smoothed down the skirt of her neat suit before glancing anxiously towards the offices.

It was ten to nine, and the car park was almost full; today the new owner of the company would be making his first official appearance. Nicola had been on holiday when the shockingly unexpected negotiations for the take-over of her employers had taken place, but her workmates had been full of gossip about what had gone on.

It was well known locally that Alan Hardy, the owner of the small building firm, had virtually lost interest in the business following the tragic death of his son, but no one had expected that he would sell out to someone from outside the area, to someone, moreover, to whom apparently the acquisition of their small local company was merely another addition to his growing business empire.

Her own job was safe enough, or so she had been assured. She had worked for Alan as his secretary-cum-PA ever since she had returned from the city over eight years ago, and very much enjoyed her work, even though lately she had found herself having to double-check almost everything her boss gave her to do.

Some of the staff were angered by the way Alan had kept the take-over a secret from them; she herself had known nothing of what was going on but, instead of anger, she felt sympathy both for Alan and for his wife, Mary.

The death of their son in a car accident had destroyed their lives and their hopes for the future. It was only natural that Alan should have lost heart…lost interest in the business.

She sighed faintly to herself. She had been feeling reasonably confident about her ability to work in harmony with her prospective new boss, whom she had been informed would probably put a manager in charge of the day-to-day running of the firm, only actually visiting them himself once a week, so that in effect she would be working for the manager he appointed; but over the weekend, Gordon, her boyfriend, had expressed unflattering doubts about her suitability as the right kind of secretary for a high-flying entrepreneur.

His comments had made her angry, but she had suppressed her feelings. Gordon was the kind of man who had a rather old-fashioned attitude towards women. Nicola blamed his mother for that. She was one of those women who, while appearing to be helpless and clinging, was in fact extremely manipulative and domineering.

Depressingly, she was beginning to be conscious more and more these days that the time she spent with Gordon often left her feeling irritated and at odds with him.

They had known each other almost all their

lives, although it was only in the last two years that they had started seeing one another on a regular basis.

At Christmas, Gordon had made noises about them considering getting engaged, but she had avoided the issue.

The trouble was that living in such a small community made it difficult for a single woman to enjoy a varied social life without the addition of a male partner.

Single women over the age of twenty-five and under the age of thirty were looked upon with a certain degree of suspicion by some of the local die-hards.

Nicola had her women friends, of course—girls she had been at school with who had since married and produced families—and, if she was honest, she preferred the fun she had in their company to the often dull dates she had with Gordon.

Her mother had already commented rather drily that a lifetime of Gordon might seem a very long time indeed, and Nicola was inclined to agree with her, but Gordon represented respectability and old-fashioned morality, and she had her own reasons for believing that she needed those attributes in her life—that Gordon, no matter how dull and boring he might be, no matter how difficult she might find it to get on with his mother, was someone she was very, very lucky to have in her life.

As she walked towards the office-block, pleasantly acknowledging the 'good mornings' of the men in the yard, while ignoring the way they looked at her legs, she reflected uncomfortably that, like her clothes, her relationship with Gordon was part of her life—not because it gave her pleasure but because it made her feel safe.

She was well past the men now, but just as she was about to open the door to her office-block she heard one of them laughing.

Immediately her face flushed. She had no idea what might have provoked their laughter; it might not even have been her, but the instant she heard it she wanted to run…to hide herself away somewhere.

It was ridiculous, this burden she carried, which she could never allow herself to put down, and all because of one mistake, one silly adolescent error of judgement… It didn't matter how many times she tried to reason with herself that that one mistake did not mean she had to punish herself for the rest of her life; she had never been able to put it out of her mind and ignore it.

In her moments of deepest despair and misery she even wondered if it might not be worthwhile trying to talk to someone about it; but then the old, familiar panic would come back, and she would remember how hard she had worked to make sure that no one, but no one knew what she had done, how hard she had worked to make sure that no one, especially no man who looked at her, could ever, ever possibly think of her as the kind of woman who…

She realised as she hurried towards her office that she was actually physically trembling.

Of all days, why on earth did she have to pick today to start worrying about the past? Today she needed to be at her most alert, her most efficient, her most impressive. The one thing she had heard about the new man was that there was no room in his organisation for the unproductive or un-committed worker. He had very high standards, apparently, and expected those who worked for him to match them.

Needless to say there had already been a ground swell of mutterings among the workforce about the potential havoc he could wreak.

Nicola didn't need anyone to tell her that the firm wasn't very productive, that its profits were very, very small indeed; or that its workforce was not efficiently deployed…that the foreman in charge of the men often turned a blind eye to certain malpractices which were expensive to his employers. The only reason they were still in business was really because in this rural area they were the only reasonably large builders around.

Their small market town served a large country

area, and until very recently there had simply
not been the business potential to attract any
competition.

Now, though, things were changing; people
were moving into the area and buying up old
property, empty farms and barns, and Nicola suspected that, if they had not been taken over, a
rival firm would soon have set up in business,
putting them into liquidation.

Many of the other employees, though, either
failed to accept or did not want to accept this, and
consequently the fact that the firm had been
taken over was a cause of much resentment.

The new man had been described to Nicola as
'full of himself, a real townee, smart as paint'.

Only a couple of her co-employees had had
anything good to say for him; one of them was
her assistant, a pretty eighteen-year-old fresh out
of college, who had told her enthusiastically that
Mr Hunt was really good-looking for someone
so old, and that, if it wasn't for her Danny, she
might have quite fancied him.

Nicola had laughed a little at this. She knew from what Alan had told her that Matthew Hunt was, in fact, not yet thirty-five years old.

Not just what one would expect, was how Alan had described him. 'A shrewd businessman, but unconventional…'

He certainly was shrewd. Her own father had confirmed that. He was in banking in the City, preferring to commute to and from his office rather than to live somewhere more urban, and it had been he who had filled Nicola in with all the background details of her new employer's professional life. Not much was known about his private life other than the fact that he wasn't married.

One of her own married friends had teased her about this, remarking, 'Well, he can only be an improvement on Gordon. Heavens, Nicki, love! He's so boring it just isn't true. I mean, these days we all know that there's more to a good and enduring relationship than world-shattering, exciting sex. Real reliability is one thing, but Gordon is another. And as for his mother…'

Nicola had been forced to laugh. Anna wasn't known for her tactfulness, and tended to say what she thought. Nicola hadn't been offended; she knew that her friend meant well although, as far as she was concerned, the idea of her new boss as a possible source of new romance in her life was completely out of the question.

And anyway, from what she had heard about him, he was the kind of man who no doubt liked the women he dated to be of the high-profile, physically attractive type, which she most certainly was not.

As she hurried into the cloakroom, she gave her reflection a hasty, disapproving glance in the small mirror.

She wasn't very tall, five feet four, with a slender frame, delicate wrist and ankle bones. From her mother she had inherited her fine pale skin and her dark hair, and from her father her surprisingly deep blue eyes.

It was an unusual combination, and one which, together with the delicacy of her facial bone-structure and the soft, feminine fullness of her mouth, earned her second and even third glances from appreciative males.

Those members of the male sex who knew her, though, soon learned that the apparent sensuality of her face and figure were not borne out by her manner.

'Repressed' was how some of the more unkind ones described her, generally after their advances had been rebuffed. Others, less critical and without a wounded ego to add malice to their comments, said she was rather quiet and withdrawn.

Nicola knew quite well what men thought of her. She didn't mind, though; in fact, she preferred them to think of her as prim and unavailable…

Once things had been different. Once she— She swallowed hard, snatching up her bag and heading for the door. It was five to nine and she had far more important things to worry about than the past.

LATER SHE WAS to wonder if she might not in some odd way have been touched by precognition—by an awareness that logic and reason had refused to allow her to entertain… But that was later, when it was much, much too late for her to take evasive action…for her to listen to the warnings the airwaves were carrying to her.

Although all the legal requirements of handing over the business had now been satisfied, Alan, her boss, was actually physically handing over control to Matthew Hunt this morning.

There was going to be a small, brief ceremony when he introduced him to the rest of the staff, and this ceremony was scheduled for ten o'clock.

It had been her suggestion, and one which had caused Alan to ponder and consider before agreeing that it would perhaps be a good idea.

When she opened the door to the small office she shared with Evie, the younger girl was already seated at the switchboard. She smiled warmly at Nicola when she walked in and, jerking her head towards the inner door, told her, 'Alan arrived a few moments ago. He doesn't look too good. I offered to make him a cup of coffee, but he refused.'

Unlike her, Evie was wearing a brilliantly coloured T-shirt teamed with a pair of equally bright shorts. Her blonde hair was caught up on the top of her head in a cluster of untidy curls, and the bright fuchsia plastic earrings she was wearing clashed horrendously with her scarlet lipstick.

The two of them could not have presented more of a contrast, Nicola recognised wryly.

Evie at eighteen looked as bright and colourful as a parrot, while she, at twenty-six, in her plain navy suit, her crisp white blouse, her neat beige tights and navy pumps, her hair cut in a classic shiny bob, looked as dull and plain as—as a secretary *ought* to look, she told herself firmly, ignoring the faint lowering of her spirits that comparing herself with Evie suddenly brought her.

'He hasn't arrived yet,' Evie told her conspiratorially. 'I wonder what kind of car he drives… Something big and posh, you can bet—probably sporty, too. He's certainly going to perk this place up a bit… Danny was saying last night that we'll see some action now.'

Danny, Evie's boyfriend, worked for the firm as well, as a trainee carpenter. His clothes were almost as colourful as Evie's, although, like her, he was an enthusiastic and hard worker.

Collecting the post, and pouring Alan a cup of coffee from the jug which Evie had just made, Nicola walked through into her boss's office.

Her heart sank as she saw him. These last two years since his son's death had taken their toll. He looked what he was—a man who had lost all purpose and motivation in his life. Nicola also suspected that he had begun to drink more than was good for him. There was a drawer in his desk which was always kept locked, and sometimes when she walked into the room there was a sour sharp smell of alcohol on the air.

She felt heartsore for him, only able to guess at how it must feel to have suffered that kind of tragedy.

Tom, his son, had been twenty-two years old and just on the point of leaving university. He had been an intelligent and well-liked young man, and the accident which had killed him had been so meaningless that it was no wonder Alan was even now unable to accept what had happened.

The driver of the other car had been drinking… had crossed the centre of the road, to plough right into Tom's car, killing both Tom and himself outright. There was no easy way for any parent to accept something like that, and now the business which should have been passed on to Tom had been sold to someone else.

'I've called a meeting of the workforce for ten o'clock,' Nicola reminded her boss as she put down his coffee in front of him.

'Luckily the men are all working locally on the house in Duke Street, and although we're paying them for it I've arranged that they will take an early lunch-hour to attend the meeting…'

The contract for renovation of a house just outside the town centre, work they were doing for a local estate agency which was moving from its existing modern premises to this much older and far more attractive property, carried stiff

penalty clauses for failure to meet time requirements. Privately Nicola thought that, in view of
the notorious tardiness of their foreman, the
penalty clauses were going to make the contract
unprofitable to them, and suspected that in ac-
cepting it Alan was betraying just another indication of how Tom's death had affected him.
When she had first come to work for him, he had
had his finger firmly on the pulse of the business,
with everything under his control. Now things
were different, and she often found she was
gently having to point out to him various pitfalls
in the contracts they took on, almost to the point
where *she* was often the one redrafting the contracts to make sure that they were actually going
to be profitable to them.

The only place which could accommodate all
of the firm's employees was an empty storage
shed adjacent to the office-block, and it was here
that the staff were going to gather to officially
meet their new boss.

From the window of her office, Nicola had a

clear view of the yard and of everyone who came and went in it, and so at ten to ten, when a battered looking Land Rover was driven noisily into the yard, she gave vent to a small sigh of exasperation.

A potential client, much as his or her business was needed, was not someone who could be properly dealt with right now, with their new owner about to arrive at any moment.

The Land Rover was mud-splashed and had at one time or another been involved in some kind of minor accident. It looked very much like any local farmer's vehicle.

It stopped right in front of the office-block and the driver got out.

He was tall, with broad shoulders encased in a windbreaker jacket, his jeans dusty and well-fitting, a pair of battered trainers on his feet. His hair was thick and dark, not black, more a rich, warm brown, growing a bit too low into his collar. His hand, she saw as he slammed the Land Rover door, was brown from constant exposure to the elements.

And then he turned his head, and in doing so caused Nicola's entire world to turn upside-down, her body frozen with shock, her entire life-force numbed by the sight of him.

No. It wasn't possible...it couldn't be possible. It was a mistake. She was wrong... It couldn't possibly be the same man. After all, it was all of eight years ago...and she had only seen him then in the half-light, and only on that one occasion...

But it was him. She knew there was no mistake...knew there could be no way she would ever make a mistake about a thing like that. And besides, she hadn't only recognised him with her eyes, but with her senses as well, each one of them reacting betrayingly to him...each one of them remembering. She shuddered inwardly, wanting to close her eyes, wanting to block out his image, odd, panicky flashes of memory swamping her...

Men when drunk did not make careful or con-siderate lovers—that was received opinion. They were careless, thoughtless, unskilled and lacking in awareness of their partner's needs or wants. That was what one always heard, but he—this man—had been different…had left her—

She shuddered again, causing Evie to stare anxiously at her and ask, 'Are you OK? You've gone dreadfully pale.' She came over to Nicola's desk, and then, as her attention was caught by what was going on outside, commented excitedly, 'That's him… The new boss… Matthew Hunt. He's arrived then… You'd better warn Alan.'

Matthew Hunt? *This* was Matthew Hunt? Nicola had to grab hold of her desk to keep her knees from buckling beneath her. *Impossible!* It couldn't be. It must not be. Matthew Hunt. Her new boss. The same man who…

She swallowed hard as the full horror of the situation hit her, her mind in complete turmoil as she sought frantically for something to hold on to, something to stop her from drowning in her own terror.

What if he recognised her? What if he…? But

no. That was impossible… He had only seen her the once, her hair had been longer then, and she had just had that dreadful disaster of a perm which had left her looking like something out of a horror film. She closed her eyes, shuddering deeply, trying not to remember how she had looked that night…the dress she had worn, bought in a fierce, reckless mood of defiant misery…the make-up she had put on…the way she had behaved… No. He wouldn't recognise her. Her own parents wouldn't have recognised her…

Her heartbeat was returning to normal, her body still tense, wary. She could hear Evie excitedly telling Alan that Matthew Hunt had arrived. Any minute now he would be walking into the office—*his* office. When he did she must be ready…prepared. She must—

She took a deep breath. The office door opened and he stood there, looking at her.

It shocked through her, as he studied her, how familiar everything about him was, right down to the piercingly intelligent way he was watching her…just as though he was somehow not quite a part of the general run of the human race…as though somehow he was elevated from it…superior.

She remembered how she had noticed that about him that night—that and, of course, his spectacular good looks, his very obvious maleness…

'Miss Linton?'

It was a statement, not a question, and she responded to it automatically, saying a little shakily, 'Yes, I'm Nicola Linton, Mr Hunt.'

The smile he gave her wasn't kind or warm.

'Make it Matt,' he told her coolly. 'Outdated lip-service to respect, when it's sycophantic and not genuine, isn't something which appeals to me…'

His comment shocked her out of her personal terror, making Nicola stare and frown.

He hadn't recognised her, she knew that, but it was evident from his manner towards her that he was not well-disposed to her. Her eyelashes flickered defensively; she knew she was not popular with the male workforce, who made fun of her behind her back and laughed about her primness, but better that than— She swallowed hard. This man was going to be her boss. Unless she gave up her job, which she did not want to do, she was going to have to find a way of getting on with him. Jobs weren't easy to come by out here, and she had no wish to commute to the city, and certainly no wish to move there. Whatever had caused his antipathy towards her, it certainly wasn't the past… She was safe from that horror, at least.

As she made some inane comment, she was aware of being in a state of intense shock, of speaking and moving automatically, as a means of defence, while really all she longed to do was to turn tail and run just as far and as fast as she could from the man watching her.

Out of the corner of her eye, she saw Alan coming out of his office. Evie beamed enthusiastically at Matthew Hunt, who gave her a surprisingly warm smile.

A sensation unlike anything she had ever experienced before seemed to pierce right through Nicola. It was like being stabbed, and she almost gasped out loud with the shock of it. To her disbelief she realised that the obstruction clogging her throat felt like a hard ball of tears... Tears, when she hadn't cried since—since she was eighteen years old... Evie's age. But at Evie's age she hadn't had one tenth of her confidence, her belief in herself as a woman...a person, even.

She turned away, blinking rapidly, clenching her hands and gritting her teeth as she willed herself to control her stupid reaction.

Tears because a man treated her with coolness and uninterest while smiling warmly and appreciatively on Evie... Why, for heaven's sake? Especially when the man in question was *this* man. Hadn't she learnt anything from the past? Hadn't all these years of living with the burden of her own guilt taught her anything—anything at all?

'It's almost ten o'clock. I believe we have a meeting to attend... I want to keep it as short as possible. There's a good deal of work to be done, and I've got a meeting in the City this afternoon…'

Silently Nicola walked towards the door. Her legs felt horribly weak, her head as though it were stuffed with cotton wool. As she reached the door, Matthew Hunt opened it for her. She made to walk past him, her body tensing, the fine hairs on her skin standing up on end as she drew closer to him. He was watching her closely. She could feel tiny beads of perspiration breaking out on her skin, but she refused to give in to the dangerous urge to turn her head and look back at him just to make sure that she was right that he hadn't realised…recognised… And then mercifully she was through the door, with Evie behind her, Evie's high heels clattering on the wooden floor.

All through the meeting she found it impossible to concentrate on what was going on.

Matthew Hunt, their new boss!

Even now she could hardly take it in. Matthew Hunt, their new boss, was the same man who…

'Are you sure you're OK?' Evie pressed her. 'You still look dreadfully pale.'

'I'm fine,' Nicola lied hollowly. 'Just fine…'

SHE SAID MUCH the same thing to her mother later in the day when she returned home from work and was asked how her first meeting with her new boss had gone.

It wasn't true, of course. All day she had been desperately conscious of the fact that Matthew Hunt was watching her, assessing her. She felt anything but fine. She suspected, from the questions he had subjected her to during the day, that he believed she had taken far too much of the day-to-day running of the firm on to her own shoulders, and he had given her the impression that under his control the company would be very, very differently run.

She could have explained to him that it had not been any desire for self-glorification or self-importance that had motivated her; that she had acted simply out of compassion and concern— but pride had kept her silent. Pride and a certain bitter stubbornness... He had misjudged her once before, and now he was doing the same thing again, and it made not one bit of difference that on both occasions, for different reasons, *she* was really the one who had been responsible for his misconceptions.

A new manager would be appointed to take over the running of the company by the end of the week, he had told her; until then, Alan would remain in charge in an advisory capacity.

Matthew had only stayed a handful of hours but, by the time he had left, Nicola had felt as wrung out and exhausted as though she had worked intensively and without sleep for a full week.

There was no doubt that professionally he was both dynamic and very, very well-informed. She could understand after listening to him just why he was so successful, but his success, his dynamism, weren't the root cause of her tension.

And she could hardly tell her mother just what it was about him that disturbed her so much.

'Oh, by the way, Gordon rang. He said to tell you that he had to cancel tonight. Apparently his mother isn't feeling too well.'

Heroically her mother managed to keep her voice light and uncritical, but Nicola already knew her parents' opinion of Gordon and her relationship with him. They had been going to play tennis this evening, but she was not sorry their date was cancelled.

'I think I'll have an early night,' she told her mother wanly. 'I feel rather tired.'

'A good long walk would do you more good than an early night… Too much sleep can cause depression,' her mother told her firmly.

Nicola managed a weak smile. Her mother was always forthright and open in her comments—unlike Gordon's mother, who was exactly the opposite.

'Maybe you're right,' she agreed.

'I am, and what's more you can take that fat, lazy dog with you,' she told Nicola.

Both of them looked at the placid labrador warming herself in front of the Aga.

Nicola laughed again.

'I see. It's not me who needs the walk, it's Honey…'

'It will do you *both* good,' her mother reiterated firmly.

A COUPLE OF HOURS LATER, leaning on a gate studying the pastoral view in front of her, Nicola reflected that, while physically the walk might have done her good, mentally… She glanced down to where Honey was lying at her feet.

Until today she had thought she had put it all behind her; that the past was the past and that she was safe from it. Now she knew she was wrong.

It had been at her own insistence that she had left home to work in the city and to share a flat with three other girls from college. Her parents had thought her too young, but had given way when she'd pointed out that at eighteen she was legally an adult.

She had found a job with a firm of City architects; she had been the youngest girl there. She had felt shy and out of place with the other girls, who were all in their twenties and who to her seemed so sophisticated and worldly… And then she had met Jonathon.

Jonathon was the son of the firm's head partner. He was being groomed to take over his father's position. He was twenty-six years old, tall, fair-haired, all smooth charm. She had been dazzled by him…awed and bemused, and of course she had fallen in love.

Naïvely she had believed he had fallen in love too, and then had come the fateful day she had overheard the conversation which had changed the whole course of her life.

Nicola closed her eyes and gave a deep shudder.

In front of her the peaceful view had faded, and once again she was standing in the small, dusty stationery-room at Mathieson and Hendry.

CHAPTER TWO

'OF COURSE I'm not interested in her, sweetheart… How can you even think it?'

Nicola froze. She had recognised Jonathon's voice instantly, and the shock of hearing him speaking to someone else in that soft, caressing voice she thought he kept specially for her, the shock of hearing him addressing someone else as 'sweetheart', held her rigid where she was, the copy paper the head of the typing pool had sent her to get clasped tensely in her arms as she stood rooted to the spot.

Jonathon was standing in the corridor, just outside the stationery-room. Obviously he had no idea she was in here, but Susan Hodges knew… She must have known because she had been there when Mrs Ellis told Nicola to come and get the copy paper.

'Well, you've been taking her out,' she heard Susan saying now.

'Only because you weren't available, my sweet. Oh, come on, honestly now. Can you really imagine that I'd be interested in someone as sexless and boring as that dull little prude? Heavens, she doesn't even know how to kiss properly… Not like you!'

Nicola heard the sound of laughter, followed by the unmistakable sound of two people kissing.

She felt both sick and angry at the same time, so desperately unhappy that she had to clench her fists to stop herself from crying, and so furiously angry both with Jonathon and with herself that if she had had to confront him right now she would probably have hit him.

How stupid she had been to believe that Jonathon actually liked her, respected her, loved her, when in reality he and Susan Hodges… Susan Hodges, the office bimbo, the pretty, pouting blonde who always wore her clothes just that little bit too tight, who always seemed to giggle just that little bit too loudly and for too long.

If anyone had told her that Jonathon was involved with Susan she would have denied it instantly and immediately, claiming that Susan simply wasn't Jonathon's type.

How naïve she had been.

'So you won't be taking little Miss Prim and Proper to the party tonight, then, will you?' she heard Susan saying to Jonathon.

He laughed.

'Hardly. I bet you've got something spectacular to wear, haven't you, Susie? Something stunning and sexy…?'

'You'll just have to wait and see, won't you?' Susie replied provocatively, adding, 'Of course, you could always come round to my place and have a private view…'

They were both laughing as they moved off down the corridor. Inside the stationery-room, Nicola remained frozen with misery.

It was true that Jonathon had not specifically invited her to partner him at tonight's party to celebrate his father's birthday, but she had assumed…had believed… She had even bought herself a new dress for the occasion. She had bought it at the weekend, having enlisted the advice and support of her mother, anxiously determined that Jonathon shouldn't be ashamed of her.

The dress in question was prettily understated, in dark blue velvet with a neat round collar and long sleeves, and suddenly, bitterly she knew that in it she would look just as sexless and boring as Jonathon had claimed she was. Tears blurred her eyes. She felt sick with shock and a bitter, burning rage, possessed by a need to show Jonathon—to show *everyone*—that she was not the dull, boring person they obviously all believed her to be, that she could be just as exciting…just as glamorous…just as desirable as the Susans of this world.

LATER she was to wonder if she had been overcome by some kind of mental instability to have reacted the way she had; certainly she had never done anything like it before, and nor was she likely to do so afterwards.

All she could think was that the pain of knowing what Jonathon really thought about her, the trauma of coming down off her cloud and crashing painfully hard back to reality, had mentally unhinged her in some sort of way.

The celebration of the fiftieth birthday of the firm's main partner was a major event within the small City firm. A room had been hired at a very grand city-centre hotel for the occasion. There was to be a buffet meal followed by dancing and, although she had tried not to show it, Nicola had been nervously excited about the event ever since Jonathon had started taking her out.

Both his parents would be there, of course, and his sisters, and in her cloud-cuckoo dream-world she had somehow or other envisaged herself being introduced to them…sitting with them… being accepted by them as Jonathon's girlfriend. Now abruptly she was realising how idiotic those daydreams had been and, in some sort of confused way, she didn't know now whether she hated Jonathon or loved him. All she did know was that she was determined to show him just how wrong his cruel comments had been, just how desirable she *could* be... Much, much more desirable than the likes of Susan Hodges.

All the staff were being given the afternoon off in order to prepare for the party. It was almost lunchtime now and, just as soon as she was sure that Jonathon and Susan were out of earshot, Nicola emerged from the stationery-room and hurried back to the typing pool with the copy paper.

For what was left of the morning Nicola's thoughts were very far from her work. She was mentally busy making plans, taking decisions and, just as soon as she was able to do so, she collected her coat and hurried out into the street.

The firm's offices were right in the centre of the City, in the banking and business area, within easy walking distance of the shops.

Thanks to the prudent teachings of her parents, Nicola already had a healthy bank-account balance, and luckily when she'd come out this morning she had brought her cheque book with her.

There was a hot, burning sensation in her chest, a fiery, driving sense of determination motivating her, pushing her... Without giving herself time to hesitate, she rushed into the very modern hairdressing salon which had recently opened close to the office.

It wasn't a bit like the hairdressers at home— no pink, no frills, the décor all stark greys and blacks, the walls adorned with huge, blown-up, unrecognisable photographs which she presumed were of hairstyles.

The receptionist behind the desk had very short, very shocking pink hair, and a supercilious stare.

Before she could change her mind, Nicola told her what she wanted. Ten minutes later she was confronting the stylist, who was asking her thoughtfully, 'You are really sure about this...?'

Nicola could feel herself starting to bristle, sensitively knowing what he was really saying—that he couldn't see someone as dull and boring as her sporting such a modern, innovative hairstyle…

'If you can't do it…' she challenged.

He frowned at her.

'Oh, I can do it, it's just that it is a radical change.' He gave her an odd look, and said quietly, 'Look, it's none of my business…but you really do have very pretty hair. A little bit old-fashioned maybe—straight hair isn't really in right now—but to have it all permed…'

Nicola gritted her teeth. She knew exactly what she wanted and she was determined to have it. She remembered seeing the photograph in the salon window on her way to work a few days ago. In it the model, dark-haired like herself, had sported a mass of tumbled, wild curls that had given her—even to Nicola's innocent eyes—a sexuality that virtually hit the onlooker between the eyes. No girl…no woman with that kind of hairstyle could ever, ever be described as dull, boring…and certainly not as sexless.

'I want it,' she told the stylist desperately.

Three hours later, staring at her transformed reflection in the mirror, she felt her heart sink. She scarcely recognised herself, and as for what her parents would say… Was her face really so tiny, so small that it looked swamped by the heavy mass of her hair, its volume virtually trebled by the intensity of the perm?

The stylist was watching her gravely, but she refused to let him see how shocked and dismayed she felt.

Gravely she studied her reflection, ignoring the pallor of her face and the hugeness of her eyes.

Equally gravely she paid the bill and collected her coat.

Once out in the street she felt oddly queasy and light-headed, but she ignored this feeling, heading for one of the nearby department stores.

The girl in charge of the trendy make-up counter she headed for pursed her lips and studied her critically when she told her what she wanted.

'Red lipstick…yes, definitely red lipstick…

with your mouth it will look terrific. The look this year is for pale skin, so you're in luck, but we'll have to do something to bring out your eyes.'

Half an hour later, Nicola emerged from her hands and fought against the impulse to run her tongue over her lips and lick off the gooey lipstick that felt as though it was plastered on them inches thick.

As she caught sight of herself in a nearby mirror, she did a double-take, barely recognising the wild-haired creature with the dark eyes and glossy, pouting mouth as herself.

Sexless was she? she asked herself grimly as she took the escalator up to the clothes department.

Firmly she ignored the section where she would normally have shopped, heading instead for the store's more 'way-out' clothes.

'Minis are back in,' the assistant told her when she explained she wanted a dress for a party. And she was lucky enough to have the legs to take them…and the figure to wear the stretchy, clingy number in eye-popping purple crêpe, which she assured Nicola was an absolute must for any girl hoping to be taken seriously as socially acceptable among her peers.

It was the same angry wave of bitterness and pain that had carried her into the hairdressers that carried her back to the flat armed with her new purchases and her new image, determined to prove to Jonathon just how wrong about her he was.

When she got back she discovered that she had the flat to herself.

Her shopping had taken rather longer than she had anticipated, and all she had time for now was a very quick shower and a bite of food.

Despite all her care, the bath seemed to leave her hair looking even more wild and tangled than it had done when she'd first left the salon.

She eyed it uncertainly, wondering if perhaps the perm hadn't been just a little bit too much of a change, and then sternly forced herself to remember Jonathan's cruel condemnation of her. No one looking at her now would consider her

sexless, would they? She looked…and looked…
A little uncomfortably, she decided she wasn't
quite sure what she looked like, other than it
wasn't really herself…

It took her a good hour and several unsuccess-
ful attempts before she managed to reproduce
something approaching the sales girl's artisti-
cally applied make-up. The blue kohl pencil certainly did make her eyes appear an extraordinary
colour, but she still wasn't sure that quite so
much lipstick—

Sternly reminding herself of what this was all
about, she ignored her own feelings of discom-
fort and struggled into her new dress.

It was odd how something so insubstantial
could make her slender body appear positively
voluptuous, even if she wasn't quite sure that
purple really was her colour.

There, she was ready.

Even the driver of the taxi she had booked to
take her to the party did a double-take when
she opened the door. She lifted her head a little

higher and gave him what she hoped was a cool stare.

Just wait until Jonathon saw her. So he thought she was dull, did he? Dull and boring and sexless… Well, tonight she was going to make him regret every single one of those unkind criticisms.

It was only when she was paying off the taxi driver outside the hotel and seeing her fellow employees arrive in groups, even worse, couples, that she realised that the very best way to show Jonathon just how wrong he was about her would be for her to turn up at the party with another man… But the problem was that she didn't know any other men—not here in the city—and certainly none of her male friends at home could hold a candle physically to Jonathon.

He was so very good-looking, so very sophisticated, so very charming… A charm that meant nothing—nothing at all, she reminded herself bitterly, ignoring the startled look of recognition from one of the other girls from the typing pool who was approaching the main doors to the hotel just as she stepped towards them.

'Nicola? It is you, isn't it? Heavens! Is that…is that a wig?' she asked Nicola uncertainly.

'No, it's a perm,' Nicola told her shortly.

She had never particularly liked Lisa. She was another blonde like Susan Hodges. Nicola's chin tilted defiantly as she saw the way the other girl was studying her appearance. Her male companion was staring at her as well, Nicola recognised, and he was staring at her in a manner with which she was not familiar. It made her feel both uncomfortable and uneasy, but she ignored these feelings, concentrating instead on the cruelty of the words she had overheard earlier in the day.

The foyer of the hotel was busy with people coming and going. A board just to one side of the reception desk had written up on it which functions were taking place in which suites, and it was easy for Nicola to find her way to the suite where their own party was taking place.

In point of fact she was familiar with the

layout of the hotel, having eaten there and attended several functions with her parents over the years.

The gloomy dimness of the room made her blink a little when she first entered it. Individual tables had been set up around the small dance-floor, and she quickly headed for one occupied by some of the other girls from the typing pool.

All of them commented on the change in her appearance, but only one of them was unkind enough to remark that she was surprised to see her turning up on her own.

'I thought you'd be coming with Jonathon,' she added pointedly.

Now Nicola was glad of the gloom. She turned her head away and shrugged her shoulders, feigning nonchalant uninterest.

But uninterest was the last thing she actually felt when Jonathon walked in with Susie on his arm.

The two of them seemed to take a long time to walk across the room. Jonathon never even looked in her direction, Nicola noticed dispiritedly, but Susie certainly did, her eyes widening a little as she took in Nicola's altered appearance.

Let her stare, Nicola thought defiantly, giving her head a bitter little toss. Let them both stare…

She was determined that, before tonight was over, she was going to make Jonathon eat his words, although it was becoming increasingly obvious to her that if she was actually to achieve this objective what she really needed was to have some other man paying attention to her, making it plain that he did not consider her either dull or sexless… And not just any man… It would have to be a very special kind of man, the kind of man who—

Her eyes widened, her breath catching in her throat as she stared at the man who had just walked into the room.

Unlike the other male guests, who were all wearing formal suits, this man was dressed casually, his soft blue shirt open at the throat, his jeans clinging to his thighs.

'Wow! Just look at that!' one of the other girls

at the table giggled appreciatively. 'I wonder where he's come from…'

'Who knows? But one thing's for sure… He won't be staying long—not dressed like that.'

'Wanna bet?' another of the girls commented drily. 'He just happens to be one of our most important clients. I knew he'd been invited, but I don't think anyone actually thought he'd come…'

Behind her the girls were giggling and chattering excitedly about the newcomer's good looks, but Nicola wasn't paying very much attention.

A waiter came round with a tray of champagne cocktails. Although normally she didn't drink, Nicola took one, and gulped thirstily at it.

The champagne tickled the back of her throat and made her cough a little, but the delicious warm feeling that spread through her stomach after she had emptied her glass was undeniably pleasant.

She felt better, too…stronger, more confident, more determined than ever to show Jonathon just how wrong he was about her.

That she also felt decidedly wobbly when she

stood up to accept a second cocktail from another waiter was something she decided to ignore.

It was just nerves, she told herself firmly. Just nerves… After all, no one, not even someone who never drank, could get drunk on two champagne cocktails—could they?

One of the girls got up and announced that she was going to the bar. She asked Nicola what she wanted to drink and, unsure of what to ask for, Nicola quickly repeated the order given by the girl sitting next to her, although not entirely sure what a 'VAT' might be.

When the drinks arrived, the odd, oily aftertaste of hers was a little strange, but nevertheless good manners made her empty her glass.

Jonathon and Susie weren't sitting with his parents, she noticed woozily as she searched the room for them. Jonathon was in fact talking to the man in jeans while Susie simpered up to him, batting her eyelashes and smiling. He was, Nicola recognised dreamily, far, far better looking than Jonathon. He was also far, far more masculine than Jonathon, and a tiny, delicious tremor of sensation suddenly and very shockingly ran through her at the thought of being held against that hard, male chest, of being touched by those very male hands.

Without even thinking about what she was doing, she got to her feet, ignoring the muzzy, dizzying sensation in her head and the odd weakness in her legs.

She walked unsteadily across the floor, and as she approached their table she saw the way Susie clutched possessively at Jonathon's arm, her eyes widening, her scarlet nails digging into his jacket.

Jonathon had seen her now. She saw the shock register in his eyes as he looked at her, and immediately a pleasurable rush of warmth and triumph ran through her stomach. She gave him a pouting smile…the kind of smile she had seen Susie use so often, and then she tossed her head, so that her wild mane of curls bounced everywhere. The motion of tossing her head had, she realised uncomfortably, made her feel rather sick.

'Hi, Jonathon.' She ignored Susie, closing the gap between Jonathon and herself so that she could look up into the jeans-clad stranger's face. 'Would you like to dance?'

She could see the shock in Jonathon's face…hear the outrage in Susie's gasp, but she didn't care—why should she? *She* was going to show Jonathon just how wrong he was about her; she was going to show him that she was desirable, sexy…that men *did* want her.

The man was looking at her now, an extremely odd expression in his eyes. For a moment, as he studied her, they hardened and became so cold that she actually flinched, tears threatening to blur her own eyes as through the fog of alcohol and misery engulfing her she realised that, despite all her efforts, he did not find her attractive—that he was in fact going to reject her. She put a defensive hand up to her face, and started to move back from him, her cheeks flushing with guilt and humiliation. However, before she could move away his hands came out and circled her wrist, stopping her. She stared at it in confusion. She had never realised that it would be possible for a man to hold her so lightly and yet so securely. He wasn't exerting the slightest bit of pressure on her skin, and yet she knew that if she tried to pull away those lean fingers would tighten around her bones like manacles.

Shocked awareness cleared the drink-induced fuzziness from her eyes as they focused on his and saw the relentless, determined glittering in their grey depths. Too stupefied to resist, she stayed where she was, bewilderment following shock as she wondered why she felt as though she had suddenly stepped off the edge of the earth.

Was it the champagne cocktails? She pressed her free hand to her stomach uneasily as she heard her captor saying coolly to Jonathon,

'Please excuse us. It seems the lady wants to dance…'

Despite the fact that she could hear no trace of irony of emphasis in his voice, she still flushed at the sound of the word 'lady'.

'Ladies' did not dress the way she was dressed tonight…they did not wear the kind of make-up she was wearing, and they certainly did not approach strange men and ask them to dance.

She half hesitated, nervously conscious of a tremor of doubt churning her stomach, of a desire to escape not just from her captor, but from the entire situation she had created, and then she looked at Jonathon and saw the trans-fixed way in which he was regarding her, and saw also in his eyes a look of mingled anger and caution. He was annoyed because she was dancing with someone else, she recognised im-mediately, and not only was he angry, he was also afraid of saying so—afraid of challenging this man standing at her side for the right to dance with her.

He was, she realised on a fierce thrill of aware-ness, if not jealous, then certainly resentful of the other man's presence at her side.

It was working, she recognised shakily. It was actually working…her hair, her clothes, her make-up were not, after all, the disaster she had begun to think; they could not be, could they, if they were making Jonathon see her as a desirable woman—as someone he did not wish to see dancing with another man.

Elation filled her. She turned to her captor and gave him a dazzling smile. His eyes widened again before his glance flicked away from her to Jonathon and then back again.

'See you soon,' she heard him saying to Jonathon, and then, somehow or other, without her being too sure how it had happened, she was on the small dance-floor and in his arms, swaying against him in time to the slow, hypnotic beat of the music.

In fact the way he was holding her felt so comforting and safe, and the pleasant heat coming off his body made her feel so warm, that she was almost tempted to close her eyes and… She gave a small, cat-like yawn, and half stumbled as she missed a step. Instantly the arms holding her tightened.

'I think the proper place for you right now is bed, not a dance-floor,' she heard him saying in her ear.

Muzzily she lifted her head from his shoulder and stared at him. It had happened, she had been right. Men didn't care about the sort of person you were…only how you looked. It had to be true, otherwise why was this man, who had never set eyes on her before tonight, telling her that he wanted to go to bed with her, when, in all the months she had been working in the typing pool, only Jonathon had even asked her out, and then he had not made any real sexual overtures to her? And she knew why. Because he thought her sexless and boring… Well, if he had just heard what he— this man—had said to her, he wouldn't think so…

Triumph filled her blood with a warm, singing heat which, mixed with the alcohol she had consumed, had an electrifying effect on her perceptions and reactions.

Recklessly ignoring the inner voice warning her to be careful, she stopped dancing and looked up at him.

'Well, if that's what you want,' she told him breathlessly, 'and if you're sure you don't mind leaving so soon…'

'Leaving?'

Nicola frowned at the sharpness in his tone, her eyes clouded and puzzled as she looked at him.

'Do you live very far out of the city?' she asked him politely. 'Only I do have to be at work in the morning, and…'

'Nicola, why don't you come and join me and Susie…?'

Her frown deepened as she realised that the music had stopped and that Jonathon was standing next to them. She hadn't even seen him leave his table, never mind walk across the floor. Without even knowing she was doing it, as he reached out to touch her she drew back from him, instinctively pressing herself closer to her companion.

Since she was looking at Jonathon, she was unaware of the quick frown that touched the other man's face as he watched the small tableau being played out in front of him.

A drunken teenager, offering him her body, was the very last thing he wanted right now. And, for all her make-up and that impossible hair, she looked as though she was little more than a baby. If he left her here in her present state, though, he'd be leaving her to the mercy of Jonathon or another of his type. His mouth twisted cynically. She might be a little idiot, but she definitely didn't deserve that.

'Too late, I'm afraid, Jonathon,' he interrupted smoothly. 'I'm afraid that Nicki and I were just about to leave…'

Nicola gave him a startled glance. He had called her Nicki… Only her family and friends at home did that—and saying that they were leaving… There was no need now—not now that Jonathon was here and wanted her—but, before she could say anything, those lean fingers were gripping her arm, and somehow or other she discovered that she had been turned around and had her back to Jonathon, and that she was being escorted very firmly across the floor.

'Do you have a coat?' she was asked when they reached the door.

She shook her head in bemusement.

'Pity…' she thought she heard him saying wryly as he glanced down at her dress.

'Jonathon,' she protested huskily, trying to turn round.

'Forget him. He's not the one for you,' she was told firmly. 'Now come on, let's get out of here.'

A tiny shock of fear ran through her. He was obviously impatient to make love to her… Her body suddenly went very cold. What was she doing leaving with this strange man? What if…?

But if she went back now without him, Jonathon would know that he was right—that she was dull, and—and boring…and sexless.

Her captor took her down to the underground car park, still holding on to her arm as he unlocked the door to a sleek Jaguar convertible, almost bundling her into it, and then fastening the seatbelt around her and closing the door before going round to the driver's side and getting in beside her.

The car smelled luxuriously of leather, and something else—something alien and exciting. It took her several seconds to realise that the smell was him… When she did, she flushed and shivered, causing him to frown at her and demand,

'Look here, you're not going to be sick are you? Because if you are…'

She shook her head.

It was true that she did feel slightly queasy, and that her head did ache dreadfully, but she was most certainly not going to be sick. What she really wanted to do, she acknowledged, as he drove out of the car park and into the dark city streets, was to go to sleep.

No sooner had the thought formed than she was leaning her head back against the head-rest and closing her eyes.

'Right, now, if you just tell me where you live…'

Silence. Matt frowned and turned his attention from the road to his passenger, his frown deepening as he recognised that she was deeply and completely asleep. That she was, in fact, sleeping like the child she was. How much had she had to drink? Enough to make her a danger both to herself and to others. If he had had any sense he would have left her where she was. Someone there would have made sure she got home safely; or would they?

He had an early flight in the morning, and she really was an additional problem he didn't need. The trouble was, though, that he had an over-developed sense of responsibility. He suspected it came of having three younger sisters.

Grimacing to himself, he acknowledged that it really was too late to turn the car round and dump her back at the party, especially with a wolf like Jonathon Hendry cruising around. The easiest thing he could do would be to take her home with him, put her to bed in the spare bedroom, and then evict her first thing in the morning before he left for New York, when hopefully she would have sobered up enough to realise how potentially self-destructive her behaviour had been.

He made one more attempt to wake her up, knowing before he did so that he was wasting his time. It was true, she did open her eyes and focus vaguely on him, but they closed again before he could even say one word, and he could tell from the way her body slumped against him that she was already deeply asleep once again.

CHAPTER THREE

NICOLA opened her eyes and stared anxiously around the unfamiliar bedroom.

It was decorated in shades of grey and white, with a plain Roman blind at the window. The bed she was in was large, the bedding white and crisp, the duvet grey and white striped. She knew immediately that this was not a woman's bedroom, and panic shot through her; she struggled to sit up and then gasped in fresh shock as she realised that all she was wearing was her briefs.

She had no idea where she was or why. The last thing she could remember was being at Jonathon's father's birthday party. She had been dancing with someone... Someone. Her body stiffened, frantic stabs of enlightening memory piercing the grey fog that covered the previous evening's events.

She remembered drinking the champagne cocktails, seeing Jonathon with Susie… seeing him—

She groaned out loud and then shuddered. What on earth had she done? What had *he*, the strange man she had left the party with, done?

She shuddered again. She wasn't that naïve. There could have been only one reason she was here in his bed this morning. The facts were self-evident.

There was a terrible wrench of nausea in the pit of her stomach, an ache in her head that made her feel as though someone had kicked it; and yet surprisingly there was nothing else—no unfamiliar aches, no real awareness that last night she had crossed the final frontier that separated the child from the woman…no memories of the man who had been her lover, other than those she had of the events preceding their departure from the party.

As she sat tensely in the middle of the large bed, trying to overcome both her physical nausea and her mental and emotional self-disgust, the bedroom door suddenly opened.

In the daylight he seemed even larger than she remembered. He had obviously just had a shower, because his hair was slicked back and still wet, his skin still showing faint traces of moisture. He had a towel wrapped around his hips. His body was hard and muscular, a shockingly masculine dark arrowing of hair bisecting his torso.

He was, she saw, carrying a mug of something hot, but as soon as he approached the bed she instinctively shrank back from him, clutching at the bedclothes and watching him with terrified eyes.

'So you're awake… Just as well since I have to leave in half an hour. I'll drop you off on my way to the airport. I've brought you some tea. If you want any aspirin, there are some in the bathroom cabinet.'

He was so matter of fact, so casual… She could feel her own face starting to burn as he sat down on the edge of the bed and it depressed beneath his weight.

She could smell the sharp lemon freshness of his soap, see the smooth sheen of his jaw where he had just shaved. His skin looked firm and tanned, the sight of his body making her tremble and then shudder as she tried not to think about last night, about how he must have—

'If you want to be sick…'

She shook her head, biting her bottom lip in an agony of self-mortification. He was so obviously used to this sort of thing, while she…

There was a mirror on the wall opposite the bed. She caught sight of their reflections in it. No wonder he had thought she might be going to be sick, her face looked so pale, an unpleasant shade of greeny-white. She frowned, suddenly realising something, her fingers touching her bare face.

As though he realised what she was thinking, he told her drily, 'I washed it off.'

She went from white to red and shuddered, all too conscious of everything else he must have done while she had been too drunk to be aware of it.

Revulsion rose up inside her, not just for herself but for him as well.

How could he…how could any man make love to a woman while she virtually had no awareness of what was going on? But then, men weren't like women…men were different, dangerous, and if she was honest with herself she had encouraged him to think—to believe…

She had started to tremble. Out of the corner of her eye she saw him reaching towards her. Immediately she arched her back to avoid him, her eyes betraying her feelings.

Matt frowned. Surely the little idiot didn't actually think he had…? He wasn't sure whether to give her a good telling off or burst out laughing. Did she really honestly think…? He remembered how small she had felt when he'd carried her in from the car…how trustingly she had snuggled up against him. How vulnerable she had felt when he stripped off that appalling dress and then her tights, before washing her face clean of her make-up and tucking her up in his spare room. He had, in fact, treated her as matter-of-factly as though she had been one of his sisters, and now she was looking at him as though he was a potential rapist.

It would have served her right if he *had* taken advantage of her, he decided grimly, looking at her; and, if she carried on behaving the way she had done last night, that was exactly what *would* happen to her.

It didn't take much intelligence to work out what had been going on. The silly little idiot obviously had some kind of crush on Jonathon Hendry.

More fool her. Now *there* was a man who would have used the situation to his advantage without a thought for the consequences. He could see how terrified she was, and what she thought… He opened his mouth to reassure her, and then paused. Perhaps he ought to go on letting her think the worst. She looked so scared and shocked that, if he did, it might just be enough to shock her into reverting to what he suspected was her true character, and never behaving so foolishly again. It would in some ways be a cruel thing to do…but, if it stopped her from behaving with another man the way she had behaved with him last night, in the long run he would be doing her a favour.

And so, instead of telling her the truth, he put down the mug, and reached across the bed, his hands on her shoulders, as he held her firmly and asked, 'What's wrong? You weren't like this last night…'

He actually felt the shudder that went through her, and saw the sickness in her eyes, but he hardened his heart against his compassion and reminded himself that this was for her own good.

'I didn't disappoint you, did I?' he added, murmuring, 'I know it was your first time, but you seemed enthusiastic enough—especially later…'

Nicola couldn't silence the anguished moan bubbling in her throat. This was awful, unbearable…far, far worse than anything she had imagined. She had no idea he would actually talk about what had happened as matter-of-factly as though it meant nothing. But then, of course, to him it did not mean anything... To him—

She could feel the warmth of his breath against her ear, and she knew that if she turned her head—if she moved at all... She froze, locking every muscle in her body, willing him to let go of her and yet terrified of closing her eyes in case he moved, and—

'What's wrong?'

His thumbs were stroking her skin—her bare skin, the delicate friction sending two conflicting messages to her senses... The first was one of shock and fear, the second... She shivered, a little unfamiliar with the shivery tremulous sensation caused by the friction of his touch, her eyes widening in sudden betraying bewilderment as beneath the protection of the duvet she suddenly felt the tightening of her nipples. A fierce tremor seemed to run through her body from where his thumb stroked her skin to the centre of her breast.

Matt saw the anguish in her eyes and frowned. Perhaps he was taking things a little too far.

Perhaps she had already learned her lesson; and then, beneath his fingertips, he felt the tiny rash of goosebumps lifting her skin. His body reacted to it before his brain, his senses aware before his intelligence, so that as she tensed and twisted frantically against him he stopped her attempt to escape with immediate masculine subjugation, sliding one hand up to her jaw, and holding her still while he turned his head and looked down at her mouth.

He told himself later that he hadn't intended to kiss her…that he wouldn't have done so if she hadn't suddenly panicked and let go of the duvet, which he hadn't even realised she was holding, to dig her nails into his arm in an attempt to fight free of him.

The pressure of her nails he barely registered; the sight of her full, soft breasts, her nipples flushed with arousal and erect, he did, and to such an extent that his free hand was cupping one of them and his mouth was on hers before he even realised what he was doing.

If he hadn't already guessed at her innocence, her reaction to him now must have proved it. She went still with shock in his hands, her mouth trembling beneath his, and for the first time in his life he realised how shockingly tempting such innocence could be.

For the space of a heartbeat he was overwhelmed by a dangerous urge to continue what he had started, to kiss her until it wasn't just her mouth that trembled, but her whole body. To caress her until the hard, flushed points of her breasts were pressing eagerly into his hands... were begging for the moist caress of his mouth. He felt his body grow taut with excitement and need, his muscles straining as he fought to control his sexual response to her, his mind torturing him with mental images of how she would feel, how she would look, how she would sound if he were to make love to her now...to show her that there was no need for her fear...to teach her that—

She was still struggling to break free of him,

and automatically he used his weight to pin her to the bed, fighting to control both her and his own desire, so that he could explain to her that she had nothing to fear, that he had only wanted to teach her a lesson… A lesson which had gone badly wrong, he acknowledged ruefully, as she bunched up her hand into a fist and thumped him in the solar plexus.

Physically the blow didn't do any damage at all but, as he recoiled to avoid it, his towel came loose and slid free of his body.

He felt the shock run through her, and cursed under his breath as he saw the expression in her eyes. She was even more innocent than he'd imagined, and quite obviously had not had the benefit of growing up around brothers or male cousins, he reflected wryly. Any minute now she was probably going to start screaming 'rape', and all because he had wanted to show her how dangerous and ill-considered her behaviour the night before had been.

What he hadn't taken into account was his own

reaction to her. Ridiculous that an innocent with the clean-scrubbed face of a little girl, who was quite definitely not his type at all, should have such an intense and immediate effect on him, when he prided himself on his self-control.

But if he let her go now…

Sighing to himself, he took advantage of her shock to reach for one of her hands, deliberately uncurling her fingers before lifting it and placing it on his body.

Her fingers were icy-cold, their touch almost as much a shock to him physically as what he had done was to her mentally. She tried to snatch her hand away, shock burning hot flags of colour in her cheeks.

'See what you've done to me,' he told her softly. 'Shall I cancel my flight to New York, so that we can…?'

As he let go of her hand, she snatched it back, looking everywhere but at him, her voice thick and choked as she denied his suggestion.

He really had no intention of cancelling his

flight, and was hoping that the suggestion that they might have sex again would be enough to reinforce her shock and make her think once she got home that she had got off lightly.

And then, when he saw her face, he knew he had to relent and tell her the truth. She looked so sick and shocked, sitting there clutching the bed-clothes around her body, her eyes huge and dark with emotion, her body trembling.

'Look,' he began, stopping as he heard the phone ring. 'Stay right there,' he told her as he reached for his towel and secured it around his body.

The phone was in his bedroom and, as he walked out of the room to answer it, Nicola could hardly believe her luck. Another few seconds…

She shuddered from head to foot, reliving the shocking moment when his towel had slipped and she had seen— She swallowed sickly. And if that had not been bad enough, when he had taken her hand and actually placed it on his body…on that part of him…

She could hear the muted sound of his voice in

another room. Her clothes were on a chair by the window, and she realised suddenly that here was her chance to escape.

She got out of the bed, frantically pulling on her clothes, her heart racing, her body tensing every time she heard him stop speaking. But then he would start again, and eventually she was dressed and on her way to the door.

It took her several precious seconds to find the main door to what she realised was a flat and, when she did find it, it took her several more to negotiate the complicated locking system; but at last she was safely on the other side and in a small foyer off which several other doors opened. Ahead of her lay a lift and a flight of stairs. She opted for the stairs, hurrying down them, relieved to discover she was only one floor above ground level.

The commissionaire in the foyer gave her a startled glance when she almost ran past his desk and through the main doors.

Outside it was a clear bright morning. She was,

she recognised, in a suburb of the city which she vaguely remembered having travelled through on several occasions with her father.

Fortunately she had money in her handbag, and she could see a bus stop not far away. She could also see a bus approaching it, and, ignoring the angry protest of the motorist she ran in front of, she raced across the road, jumping on to the bus just as it was about to pull away.

'Dangerous thing to do that, miss,' the conductor told her disapprovingly as she paid her fare.

She started to laugh then, a high-pitched, almost hysterical laugh that caused the conductor to frown and then shrug his shoulders. These teenagers…all of them on drugs and what have you… Who could make any sense of what any of them did?

IT TOOK Nicola three days to decide that she had had enough. She endured Jonathon's taunts and goads about what had happened after she had disappeared with MH—as he referred to the man she only knew as Matt, and about whom she wished to know absolutely nothing more whatsoever—for as long as she could, and then finally, when he had accosted her in the corridor just once too often, demanding to know what had happened, and sneeringly asking her if she thought she was going to be able to keep a man like MH interested in her, she finally snapped.

The oddest thing about the whole affair was that, from the moment she had seen Jonathon on the morning after the party, she had experienced such a sense of revulsion towards him that she couldn't understand how she had ever even thought him mildly attractive, never mind wanted him enough to have behaved in such an appallingly stupid fashion.

Just how appallingly and stupidly she had behaved was something she could not bear to think about at all. Every time she recalled waking up in *his* bed…every time she remembered how he had touched her…kissed her…how he had made her touch *him*…how he had intimated that during the night they had been lovers not once but several times, she felt physically sick...*was* physically sick—at least, on the first day.

That had been another cause of guilt and anxiety. The rhythms of her body—normally so regular and orderly—quite obviously disrupted by the stress she was under, had even caused her to think for a few dreadful, agonising days that she might actually be pregnant.

Once she knew she was not, she vowed that never, ever again would she behave in such a way...that never, ever again would she try to change herself, to pretend she she was something she wasn't. And then sickeningly she realised that that was exactly what she was going to have to do, because she could not now go back to being the girl she had once been. She could not now have the same self-respect, the same belief and faith in herself. She was, she decided hollowly, a fallen woman and, as such, thoroughly deserving of any decent man's contempt and disdain. After what she had done it was no wonder that Jonathon and his ilk should assume that she was ready and willing to indulge in casual, meaningless sex.

If men treated her with disrespect and saw her as sexually available, then she had no one to blame but herself. She saw clearly now just what her impulsive behaviour had led her to. How long would it be before Jonathon would hear from Matt's own lips confirmation of all that he had said to her? She gave a deep shudder. She felt so…so filled with self-loathing and disgust, so deeply ashamed of herself.

City life wasn't for her, she decided miserably. All she wanted to do now was to go home where she could feel safe, where there would be no Jonathon, no Matt…where she could put what had happened behind her…where she could start rebuilding her life in such a way as would ensure that never again would any man ever be able to claim as Matt had—and could—that she had had casual sex with him…where no man could insult her with the insinuations that Jonathon had been making these past few days.

By the end of the week she had given in her notice, and long, long before Matt was back from New York she had left the city and was back at home.

He made enquiries, of course. Despite the complexity of the business negotiations, he had been involved in in New York, he had still found time to worry about her and to wish she had not rushed out of the flat before he had had a chance to explain what had really happened.

He pictured her worrying herself sick about the entire episode, trying frantically to remember what had actually happened. He remembered the look on her face when he had taken her hand and placed it on his body, and cursed himself for having done so.

When he did get back one of the first things he did was get in touch with Mathieson and Hendry.

In response to his carefully casual enquiry he was told that the girl in question was no longer with the company and had returned to her parents in the country, without leaving any forwarding address.

He told himself that there was really no reason for him to make any further enquiries; she had obviously learned the lesson he had wanted to teach her. He had been gone for over a month, long enough for her to have realised that there were going to be no permanent consequences from their supposed night together.

About the effect on her when she eventually discovered that she had not, as she supposed, had a lover, but was, in fact, still a virgin, he preferred not to think; pursuing her into the country to enlighten her on that point was something he didn't really think it would be wise to do, more for his own sake than for hers…

He winced a little, remembering how his body had reacted to her. It had been a long time since he had last had a serious relationship…perhaps too long. And as for the girl—Nicki—well, with a bit of luck she would have realised by now the dangers of the way she had behaved.

He smiled a little grimly to himself, reflecting wryly that, although she herself might not believe it, he *had* acted in her best interests.

He remembered the look on her face when he had kissed her…how she had felt—and then he stopped himself. There were, after all, some avenues in life which it was wiser not to go down…because they led nowhere…or because they led somewhere that was far, far too dangerous?

It was a question he preferred not to answer.

SOMEWHERE in the distance a dog barked, startling Nicola back into the present. She gave a small shiver, rubbing her upper arms with stiff fingers.

Even now, all these years later, she still could not shake off the cold horror of the moment when she had realised that she and Matt—Matthew Hunt—had been lovers, and that she could remember not one single thing about it. The shame, the anguish, the self-disgust of that knowledge would be with her for as long as she lived.

The make-up she had never used again, the dress had been thrown away, and eventually even the perm had grown out of her hair; but nothing had been able to eradicate her feeling of guilt and self-disgust.

And that was why she lived her life the way she did, keeping to the shadows, sticking firmly within the boundaries of the kind of behaviour she had set for herself, enjoying the company of her women friends, even though there were occasions when the conversation turned to sex, and they were making outspoken and sometimes rather outrageous if amusing comments about their partners, and she had to bite on her tongue and keep silent. That was why she dated someone like Gordon, who was thankfully uninterested in making sexual overtures to her.

If sometimes she woke in the night, mentally grieving for all that she was denying herself in living her life this way—the lover, the children—

she only had to recall the way she had behaved with Matthew Hunt…the sick disgust and horror that had followed the realisation that they had shared the most intimate act two human beings could share, and that she had absolutely no memory of it…to remind her of how unfit she was to encourage and accept a man's love.

It made no difference telling herself that she had only done what thousands of foolish girls did every year; others might be able to forgive her, but she could not forgive herself. Even though she knew also that her attitude, her self-denigration, was self-destructive and dangerous, and that the wisest, the most sensible course would be for her to undergo some kind of professional counselling to help her put what had happened in its proper perspective, she stubbornly refused to even consider letting go of her self-imposed punishment.

While she alone knew what had happened, she had felt reasonably safe. Now… She remembered the way Jonathon had taunted her when he had realised she had spent the night with Matthew Hunt…the insults he had thrown at her, the names he had called her…the way he had terrorised her once he'd realised that no amount of mental blackmail was going to make her allow him to have sex with her.

How bitterly she had realised then how very much more preferable it was to be considered dull, sexless and boring than to be subjected to the kind of pressure he was trying to exert. But by then it was too late…by then Jonathon had told just about everyone she worked with just what she had done.

She shivered again, and Honey, sensing her desolation, pushed a cold, wet nose into her hand, causing her to look down and give the dog a brief, painful smile.

'Oh, Honey, what am I going to do?' she whispered, kneeling down to fondle the dog's silky ears.

'If he suddenly recognises me—realises…'

She could feel the tension invading her body, the panic starting to claw at her stomach.

He wasn't *going* to recognise her, she assured herself. If he hadn't done so by now—and he hadn't, that was obvious—then why should he ever?

After all, he had probably forgotten she even existed. But if he did remember…

She shuddered deeply. The only way she could ensure that that would not happen would be to give up her job and move out of the area, to run away as she had done once before; but, like all creatures who felt hunted, she had learnt long ago that to move…to run was to attract attention, and that her best chance of safety and protection lay in the camouflage of not drawing attention to herself.

If she gave in her notice, her friends, her family would start speculating…wondering. Her parents would be anxious, and want to know what was wrong.

She could, of course, always say that there was a clash of personalities—that she could not get on with their new boss—but jobs as interesting as hers were hard to come by in this rural area, and she had no wish to start a new career in the city, no wish at all…

No, she was safe enough for now. Just as long as she kept her head…just as long as she didn't betray herself by doing something foolish.

Today, for instance, during this morning's meeting, Matthew Hunt had glanced piercingly at her once or twice when Alan in his speech had praised her for her hard work, but it had been the hard, assessing look of an employer to an employee—not the look of a man to a woman.

But then, he was hardly likely to give her that kind of look, was he? she derided herself. After all, the real her was so very different from the Nicola—the 'Nicki'—he had known so briefly.

At her feet Honey whined and pawed at her jeans-clad leg, indicating that she had had enough of sitting waiting for something to happen, and that it was time to turn around and go home.

'HAVE A NICE WALK?' her mother asked her cheerfully when she opened the kitchen door. 'Your father's just come in, so I'd better serve supper. Oh, and by the way, Christine rang. She asked me to remind you that you're having dinner with them next week…'

Nicola nodded her head. Christine was one of her oldest friends. Her husband, Mike, was a solicitor, just starting up in his own local practice. They had two small children, and, as well as looking after them, running the house, taking care of their large garden, Chrissie also helped Mike out with his paperwork at home.

They were a well-matched, happy couple, and Nicola always enjoyed the time she spent with them, even though sometimes their very evident contentment and love for one another made her feel a little envious.

Over supper her father asked her what she had thought of her new boss.

Her heart started to beat frantically fast as she looked down at her plate, knowing that if she looked up her real feelings would show far too plainly in her eyes.

Already it was beginning…the deceit…the anxiety…

'He seems very well-informed…very efficient,' she answered unevenly.

'Mm. From what I've heard he's got a nose for a good opportunity. With him behind it, the firm should really start to pick up. Will he be running it himself or—?'

'No, he's putting in a manager—someone from one of his other companies. We haven't heard who yet.'

'And this manager, you'll be directly responsible to him, I imagine?' her mother interrupted.

Nicola nodded her head. That was the one bright gleam in the whole sorry mess—the fact that Matthew Hunt would be spending a limited amount of time with them.

'I wonder how old he'll be, and if he's married…'

Nicola put down her knife and fork. She was on familiar and much safer ground here.

'Mother…' she warned.

'I'm sorry, Nicki. When you were in your teens, I promised myself I wasn't going to turn into the kind of mother who was always on the look-out for a potential father for her grandchildren, but when I look at Gordon…' She gave a small shudder and said forthrightly, 'What on earth do you see in him? And as for that mother of his—'

'Gordon is a friend, Mother…nothing more,' Nicola told her firmly.

'Mm. Still, this new manager… I wonder what he'll be like,' her mother continued, undeterred.

CHAPTER FOUR

HER mother wasn't the only one to be curious about the new manager, as Nicola discovered in the morning when she got to work.

The brief visit Matthew Hunt had paid them the previous day was not going to be repeated until towards the end of the week, she had been relieved to learn. Until then, Alan would, nominally at least, remain in charge.

Nicola had got the impression the previous day that Matthew Hunt's decision to take over the firm had been a rather impulsive one, and that he was having to shuffle around his existing staff in order to find someone responsible and whom he could trust to take charge of his new acquisition.

The knowledge of the take-over seemed to add

a new zest to the work-force. There was talk of better rates of pay and working conditions, now that they were part of a much larger organisa-tion—of bonus schemes and other perks.

Alan had opted not to have a formal retirement party and, knowing how what was happening must be reactivating the trauma of losing his son, Nicola didn't blame him. Even so, she thought it was very sad that after a lifetime of owning the firm he should simply opt to walk out of his office on Friday afternoon without any acknowledge-ment on the part of those who worked for him.

All day Tuesday there was an atmosphere of excited tension in the air. They already knew that on Wednesday morning Matthew Hunt would be introducing them to their new boss, the new manager.

Nicola, unlike everyone else, was frantically busy on the Tuesday, gently prodding Alan into going through all their current files so that she could prepare status reports on each of their current contracts, giving details of work in progress.

She loved her job, and the more responsibility Alan gave her the more she thrived on it. She had a talent for administrative work and, although few people knew it, it was mainly thanks to her ability to keep tabs on the various clients that the firm had not lost several of its major contracts.

Naturally enough, Nicola wanted to make a good impression on the man who was going to be her new boss, and not just for her own sake, but for Alan's as well. Out of loyalty to him, she was determined to make sure that he was presented with an efficient and up-to-date, as well as comprehensive run-down of exactly what was going on.

Every time she walked into his office, Alan seemed to have amassed even more paper from the filing cabinets. The shredder was going to be working overtime, she decided ruefully, looking at the dates on some of the files. Alan was something of a squirrel when it came to his files. She reminded him gently that he would have to make arrangements to have his large partner's desk removed from the office.

It was a very good antique piece of furniture, which he had bought in a sale when he had first started the firm, and she suspected it was now worth a considerable sum of money.

He gave her a wan smile.

'There won't be room for it in the bungalow; and besides...' he touched the wood gently '...where's the point?'

Nicola felt close to tears, and decided privately that, if Alan didn't do anything about it himself, she would ask her father if it was possible for them to store the desk in one of their outbuildings, because she was sure that, given time, Alan would regret abandoning it.

On Tuesday evening when she arrived home dusty and tired, her mother commented, 'You're very late.'

'Mm. We've been cleaning out Alan's office— getting ready for the new man... Has Gordon telephoned?' she asked.

She and Gordon were supposed to be attending a concert in the city, and she had half expected him to telephone to confirm what time he was picking her up.

'Not while I've been in,' her mother told her.

After she had showered off the dust and dirt and changed into a pair of jeans and a casual top, Nicola dialled the number of Gordon's mother's house.

She sometimes thought that she and Gordon were an anomaly in these modern times, in that both of them still lived at home, but then she had read several articles indicating that, because of the exorbitant cost of property, adult children were remaining in the parental home for much, much longer than had once been the norm.

Certainly Gordon, at thirty-four, might be supposed to be able to afford his own house. He had a good job with an insurance company but, as he had once carefully explained to Nicola, his mother was widowed and not very strong, and he felt he owed it to her to live with her.

She, too, could perhaps have afforded to buy her own small property, but she liked living with her parents, enjoying their company and their

conversation, even though her friends sometimes teased her about the fact that she was still
living at home.

Gordon's mother answered the telephone, her
faint, helpless whisper hardening a little when
she recognised Nicola's voice.

'Gordon is just about to eat,' she told Nicola
disapprovingly, 'so I hope you won't keep him
for too long.'

Sighing faintly, Nicola gritted her teeth.

Gordon, when he came to the phone, sounded
tense and hesitant. When she reminded him about
the concert, he paused for a moment, and then
told her quickly, 'I'm sorry, but I won't be able to
go… You see, Mother hasn't been feeling very
well and I really feel I should stay here with her…'

In point of fact Nicola hadn't particularly
wanted to attend the concert. It had been Gordon
who had suggested they go and not her, but
nevertheless when she replaced the receiver she
was seething. Why on earth hadn't Gordon telephoned her to say that the evening was off? Why

had he left it to *her* to get in touch with *him*? And as for his mother's supposed ill health…

It wasn't so much that she minded missing the concert, as she explained later to Christine when she drove round on impulse to see her friend. It was the fact that he hadn't even thought to let her know earlier that their evening was to be cancelled.

'Why on earth do you bother with him?' Christine asked her forthrightly. 'I mean, come on, Nicki, don't try telling me that he makes your heart beat faster, or that you fancy him to death—I've seen you with him.'

Nicola had to laugh. 'No, maybe not,' she agreed.

'So then, why…?' Christine began, but Nicola very firmly changed the subject and started to ask her instead how young Paul was getting on at school.

It was quite late when she got home, but she knew the evening with her friend had done her good. However, as she hovered on the point of falling asleep, her strongest feeling was one of anxiety as she worried about the morning. Not so much because of meeting her new boss, but because of Matthew Hunt.

Please God, don't let him recognise me, she prayed desperately. Anything, anything but that...

'MATTHEW HUNT'S here, but he's on his own,' Evie announced excitedly, as she came hurrying into Nicola's office.

Nicola had already seen Matthew's arrival for herself. Today he wasn't driving the ancient Land Rover, but a sleek and very expensive-looking Jaguar.

'Isn't he just the sexiest man you've ever seen?' Evie drooled as she watched him walk towards the office-block. 'I mean, just look at him...even in that stuffy suit he still looks wonderful.'

Nicola hid a small smile. The stuffy suit in question might not appeal to Evie as much as the jeans Matthew had worn on his previous visit, but it did give him an aura of power and control that made Nicola herself suddenly conscious of the *frisson* of tension that flashed hotly over her skin.

She turned away from the window, appalled by her reaction to him, only half listening to Evie's excited chatter. Evie had heard on the grapevine that Matthew's take-over would mean an updating of their office systems to include the very latest state-of-the-art technology, and she was just asking Nicola if they were likely to be using new, streamlined word processors instead of their existing electronic typewriters, when the door opened and Matthew walked in.

He smiled at Evie, causing her to blush and simper, and then gave Nicola a much sharper, considering look.

She was wearing what she considered to be her working uniform of a Prince of Wales check suit with a fine overstripe in crimson, a white shirt, and a wide crimson belt which brought out the colour of her suit.

As Evie had remarked innocently this morning, to colour-co-ordinate the outfit she should perhaps have been wearing red lipstick, but the mere thought of doing so had made Nicola feel physically sick… It had been red lipstick she had been wearing that night…

These days she stuck to a dull, work-a-day soft pink which did little more than enhance the natural colour of her mouth, and which certainly did not emphasise its soft, full contours.

So there was really no reason why Matthew Hunt's gaze should linger thoughtfully on her mouth for what to Nicola seemed like a lifetime, but which she knew could only be a handful of seconds. As he studied her, fear ripped through her. He had recognised her. He had—

'Is Alan in?' he asked her briefly.

She shook her head.

Alan had had to go out and visit a client who was complaining that they were behind schedule with their work. Loyalty to him made her keep back this particular piece of information as she explained where he had gone, but to her consternation Matthew's mouth hardened a fraction and he said immediately,

'I hope we're not on a penalty clause with that contract. We're already too far behind. Which reminds me…the foreman…Jackson…I want to have a word with him some time—'

'Would you like a cup of coffee, Mr Hunt?' Evie broke in.

The smile Matthew gave her made something wrench painfully inside Nicola. It was the indulgent, appreciative smile of an adult for a pretty child, and it struck her sharply that no man ever had, and now ever would, look at her like that.

Don't be ridiculous, she told herself sharply. She wasn't a child, she was an adult, an equal to any man, and wanted to be treated accordingly…not humoured and indulged as though she were dim-witted.

'Matthew, please, Evie,' he corrected her, reminding her that he had already told everyone that they were to address him by his Christian name.

'So when will Alan be back?' he asked Nicola.

'I'm not sure. Before lunch.'

'Mmm. Well, while I'm waiting for him, I'll go

through the work in progress sheets—if you could just get them for me, Nicola…' He paused suddenly and gave her another sharp look before walking through into Alan's office and closing the door behind him.

Once she had the appropriate sheets, Nicola took the coffee from Evie, knocked on the door, and walked in.

Matthew wasn't seated behind Alan's desk. Instead he was standing by the window looking out into the yard. Without turning his head he told her, 'Sit down, please, Nicola. There's something I want to discuss with you. Oh, and close the door, would you, please?'

Her heart started to pound with frantic fear. He had remembered her, after all, and now he was going to tell her so…to remind her of what she had done…of how she had behaved, and tell her that in the circumstances he could hardly have her working for him. She knew it.

Shakily she did as he had told her and sat down, hoping that her body wasn't trembling

visibly, betraying the intensity of the nervousness she could feel inside.

She could feel sweat starting to break out on
her skin, physical evidence of her inward panic.
She gritted her teeth and curled her hands into
tense fists as she willed herself not to lose
complete control.

'It's about Alan,' Matthew told her without
turning around. 'Nothing seems to have been
arranged to formally mark his retirement...'

For a moment Nicola was too stunned to speak.
He hadn't remembered her at all, she recognised
in shaky relief. He wanted to talk about Alan's
departure from the firm, not hers.

'Are you all right?'

She hadn't seen him turn round and walk
towards her, but now, as she saw him coming
towards her, she shrank back in her chair,
causing him to pause and frown while she stam-
mered frantically.

'Yes, yes, I'm fine. I just...' She shook her
head, trying to clear her head, to fight her way

back to normality, to dismiss her shock and deal with his query.

'Alan—Alan wanted to leave without any fuss. You'll know about his son... In the circumstances—'

'In the circumstances, some acknowledgement at least of the years he has run the firm is called for, even if it's only an apparently informal collection among the staff to buy him some memento and present him with it.'

From the tone of his voice, Nicola suspected that he was criticising her for not already having instituted something along these lines, and her fear receded, professionalism coming to her rescue as she tilted her chin and said firmly, 'Something along those lines *has* been organised.'

As soon as she had known that Alan was leaving, she had organised an impromptu collection, and with the money she had arranged that they would buy Alan a presentation hand-cut goblet with the dates of the years he had owned the company and its name inscribed on it.

All she hadn't done was arrange a time when the goblet could be presented to Alan, and as she explained all this to Matthew she added tentatively, 'Of course, I'll have to have a word with our new manager. I had thought perhaps Friday afternoon.'

'I don't see any problem with that,' Matthew assured her, 'and some kind of informal buffet meal could be organised, if it isn't too late. By the way,' he added picking up his coffee, 'there isn't going to be a new manager...at least not for the time being... The man I had in mind is having to take some sick leave.'

'So who will run the company?' Nicola asked him with concern.

He put down his cup and studied her calmly.

'I shall.'

Nicola was glad that she was already sitting down, otherwise she felt she might have betrayed herself completely.

'I think you and I will work very well together, Nicola,' she heard him adding quietly, confounding her completely as he added, 'I like your initiative, and your awareness…your compassion for your fellow human beings. Those are very valuable and necessary assets in business today, and unfortunately they are not assets which the male sex is very strong on.'

He was smiling at her now. Not the same kind of smile as he had given Evie, but it was a smile of warmth and approval, none the less, and she was shocked by the sudden burgeoning of warmth in her own heart that it gave her.

It was because he had shocked her with his concern for Alan…a concern she had never expected him to display, that was all, she told herself shakily. Yes, that odd feeling of warmth was caused by that…that and the relief of knowing he had not, after all, recognised her.

Later, as she informed Evie of what was going to happen, she told herself that, if she was going to ensure that Matthew did not recognise her, then she was going to have to stop behaving so irrationally every time he spoke to her.

As THE WEEK progressed and she worked more closely with Matthew, Nicola found herself discovering aspects of him she would never have guessed existed. Far from being the callous business type she had first imagined, she discovered that he was a very aware and concerned employer, even if he was not a man to allow anyone to take advantage of him.

He was already aware of those members of the firm who worked hard and those who did not and, although he had said nothing specific to her, Nicola suspected that it wouldn't be long before the foreman was replaced.

She liked the way he made use of her own experience and expertise, questioning her closely about their existing contracts, and listening carefully to her answers, consulting her about his proposals for expanding their customer base and discussing with her various aspects of his business as a whole so that she felt her opinions and views were valued.

In fact, if it had not been for her constantly recurring dread that he might one day remember her, she had to admit that she would have thoroughly enjoyed the challenge of working with him, and even perhaps have been regretting the fact that it was only temporary.

He had, he had told her, a very able deputy who was more than capable of taking over the day-to-day overall control of his empire while he got his new business on its feet.

'In fact it will do both Giles and me good. I'm thinking of offering him a partnership eventually. He's engaged to my youngest sister,' he added with a smile. 'Although that isn't why I want him as a partner... There comes a point where running a business like this single-handed becomes a way of life, rather than a part of one's life. I enjoy my work, but I don't want it to become my whole life. One day, hopefully, I shall marry and have children, and when I do... Well, let's just say I don't intend to be an absentee husband and father.

'Have you any plans to get married, Nicola?'

She shook her head, not trusting herself to speak. It was just as well she had the past to hold as a barrier between them, otherwise she suspected she might come dangerously close to falling into the classic trap and allow herself to become too vulnerable to his very evident appeal. By falling in love with him? Surely even without the past she was far too sensible to commit that kind of folly, even if her heart did beat ridiculously fast when she happened to look up from her work and find him watching her.

If she was ever foolish enough to imagine that the way he was regarding her meant that he was attracted to her, she only had to recall the past to realise how stupid she was being.

Of course it was possible that, following the mores of the times, his own outlook on life had undergone a change, and that he now shunned brief sexual encounters. He wouldn't be on his own in doing so, after all, but she still found it hard to reconcile the man who had so casually taken her home with him, stripped her of her clothes and then made love to her, not once but, according to him, several times, and all without her being able to remember a thing about it, with the same concerned, compassionate man who was now her employer.

ALAN WAS spending his last week with the firm going round making his farewells to some of his old customers, more at Matthew's behest than at his own instigation.

'It will keep his mind off the trauma of what's happening,' Matthew had told Nicola. 'And it will also give us time to organise the buffet luncheon for Friday. I have asked Alan to stay on in an advisory capacity. This firm has been his life, and I suspect he's going to find it very difficult to adjust to life without it.'

'He and Mary are leaving the area; they've bought a bungalow on the coast...'

'Yes, I know, and I hope it isn't something he's going to regret—moving away from an area where they've lived all their lives...from their friends.'

'They have a married daughter and they're moving to be closer to her and their grandchildren,' Nicola informed them. 'I think they're both hoping that being with their grandchildren will help to take their minds off the tragedy…'

For a moment both of them were silent, and then Matthew said slowly, 'I've often thought that must be one of life's hardest burdens to bear—the death of a child. Now, about this presentation…I take it there aren't going to be any formal speeches? You did say that Alan had said specifically that he didn't want any fuss. Do you think he would prefer it if I wasn't here…?'

His sensitivity amazed Nicola. Gordon would never have behaved like that, and he, for all his devotion to and fear of his mother, would never have dreamed of asking the advice of a woman whom he deemed to occupy an inferior professional position.

THAT EVENING, when her mother remarked how much more cheerful she had begun to look since she started working for her new boss, Nicola coloured up defensively, biting her bottom lip.

'I've heard he's very good-looking,' her mother added, apparently oblivious to her confusion.

'Very,' Nicola agreed huskily.

'And single…' her mother pressed.

'Yes,' Nicola agreed tautly, and then changed the subject, asking, 'Has Gordon phoned? We were supposed to be playing tennis this evening.'

'Not as far as I know, although I have been out for most of the afternoon.'

She was halfway towards the telephone when she stopped suddenly and turned round again. Why should she be the one to ring Gordon when he was the one who had made arrangements for them to play tennis? As she sat down again and poured herself a second cup of tea, she realised how often *she* was the one who had to get in touch with Gordon, instead of the other way round. Rebelliously she decided that this time she was going to leave it up to him.

It was eight o'clock before Gordon rang her, half an hour after he had arranged to pick her up.

As always these days when he spoke to her, his voice was edgy and defensive.

After she had accepted his explanation that he had been delayed at work, and his apology for neglecting to ring her, she reminded him, 'You won't forget that you're picking me up from work on Friday evening will you, Gordon?'

She'd booked her own car in for a service earlier in the week, and Gordon had offered to pick her up and run her to the garage to collect it.

'Of course not,' he responded in an injured voice.

After she had replaced the receiver, Nicola admitted that it was probably time their relationship was brought to an end. She certainly derived very little pleasure from his company these days, and she was beginning to suspect that he felt the same way. The very staid and not altogether enjoyable kisses they had once shared had degenerated into a perfunctory peck on the cheek, if she was lucky and, while it had been useful to have a comfortable male partner to escort her at various social functions, she was suddenly becoming aware of how very sterile and depressing she found the time she spent with Gordon.

A little bleakly she found herself comparing Gordon to Matthew… His dates, she was quite sure, were not fobbed off with excuses about the health of his mother, and arid pecks on the cheek at the end of the evening. His dates would not need to fall back on the company of girlfriends to have someone to talk to and laugh with. His dates—

Abruptly she tried to stem her dangerous thoughts. What on earth was she thinking… doing? She started to tremble, a small ache erupting deep within her body—a yearning, despairing need…emotions she had sworn she could never, would never allow herself to feel suddenly exploding inside her.

Emotions which she discovered were refusing to go away or be subdued.

THAT MORNING, she arrived at work to discover Matt frowningly standing beside her desk.

'I'm sorry. Am I late?' she began, as she walked in.

Immediately his face cleared.

'Did you think I was glowering at *you*? If so, I obviously haven't made a very good impression on you… No, I was just a little concerned about a telephone call I've had from one of our clients. It seems that Jackson has been pilfering some of the supplies from the job, or so this chap thinks.'

Ian Jackson was the foreman in charge of the men, and Nicola's heart sank. She wasn't surprised by the client's complaint, only that they did not receive more. For a long time she had had a strong suspicion that Ian Jackson was involved in the theft of supplies which she knew must be taking place, even though Alan never seemed concerned about it.

'I need to go down to the site and find out what's going on,' Matthew told her, adding, 'Are you busy here, or would you like to come with me?'

Nicola stared at him, her face flushing a little.

'It's OK, you don't have to,' Matthew told her drily. 'I just thought you might like a change from sorting through dead files…'

His reference to all the extra work she had been doing to streamline their paperwork surprised her. She hadn't known he had been aware of all the extra time she had been putting in, and his thoughtfulness now made her warm to him even more, especially when she remembered how initially, when he had first taken over the business, she had thought he was antagonistic to her. Now she suspected that that fear had sprung from her own dread of being recognised by him.

'Well, if you're sure I won't be a nuisance,' she said hesitantly.

He was looking at some papers on the desk, but now suddenly he straightened up and turned round to look at her, giving her a look which made her heart turn over and hammer against her ribs.

'I doubt that any man would ever consider you

to be a nuisance, Nicola,' he told her gravely, 'and *I* most certainly do not.'

From another man she would have considered the remark to be flirtatious, but it seemed so impossible that Matthew could be flirting with her that she could say nothing, only swallow hard, and then say huskily, 'I'll just get my jacket.'

TODAY HE WAS driving the Land Rover, and Nicola was glad that her pleated skirt allowed her to scramble up into it without having to rely on him for assistance, even though the fact that he stood politely by the passenger door to ensure that she made it safely into the seat made her feel acutely self-conscious.

She was just about to close the door when he stopped her, one hand touching her arm lightly as he leaned forward and tucked the hem of her skirt out of the way of the door.

'You've got incredibly delicate wrists and ankles,' he told her easily as he smiled into her eyes. 'There's something about that kind of fragility in a woman that makes a man feel immensely protective…'

His hand was still resting lightly against her arm, the heat of his skin burning through the fine fabric of her jacket and her blouse. Suddenly she had a shockingly clear memory of how he had held her that night at the party—of how his fingers had gripped her wrist then, of how strong she had realised he was, of how vulnerable he had made her feel, of how—

Without realising what she was doing, she flinched back from him, the colour leaving her face.

Immediately he frowned and released her, closing the door and walking round to his own side of the Land Rover.

He drove to the site in silence, while Nicola tried to control her sick trembling.

Just for a moment before, she had forgotten the past…forgotten everything but the feeling filling her as he had looked at her.

Why was she reacting to him like that? She

knew he was a very attractive man, mentally as well as physically, but she had met attractive men before without her emotions and hormones going haywire.

Or was the cause deeper and more personal? Was it because her body instinctively recognised and remembered his? Because her senses, her femininity knew him? That she…? But no. If *she* couldn't remember what had happened between them, then surely her subconscious would not remember either, and certainly not to such an extent that it was responsible for the way she was feeling right now?

It dismayed her that, after years of believing that sexually she was in full control of herself, she should suddenly start reacting like this and to this man of all men—the very man she ought not to be responding to at all.

And just because he'd paid her a compliment, just because he had for a second looked at her mouth as though… She swallowed hard. As though what? As though he wondered how she would taste…how her lips would feel beneath his…how—

Stop it, stop it! she warned herself despairingly. What was happening to her? *Why* were her own emotions turning traitor on her like this?

The Land Rover stopped, and she realised with a start that they had reached the site. She made to open the door and get out, but Matthew stopped her.

'It's a bit muddy underfoot. You might slip. Hang on a sec and I'll help you down.'

She was trembling long before he opened the door and reached inside to place his hands either side of her waist and swing her down on to the small, firm patch of ground at his feet.

CHAPTER FIVE

'ARE you all right?'

Matt's voice was curt, angry almost. She could feel the hot wave of colour burning up under her own skin as she responded equally briefly in the affirmative.

She knew that he must be regretting having asked her to come with him. What an idiotic thing for her to do. Hadn't she told herself over and over again that, if he hadn't recognised her before he was hardly likely to do so now, unless she gave him cause to do so? And yet here she was, behaving in a way that was bound to make him wonder what was wrong with her.

Ian Jackson had seen them and started walking towards them, defiant arrogance in the look he gave Matthew before stopping in front of him. The look he gave Nicola made her clench her muscles and look away from him.

She always felt uncomfortable, embarrassed and somehow guilty when she was confronted by overt male sexual appraisal, especially when it was accompanied by the kind of insulting, unspoken attitude typified by men like Ian Jackson. The way he looked at her made her want to turn and run away from him. It made her feel threatened and vulnerable, and in some way as though something about her, something she had done, was responsible for his attitude towards her…like a rape victim believing that in some way she herself had encouraged her attacker without knowing how she might have done so. Nicola knew that this fear was directly attributable to the night she had met Matthew for the first time, and that it had its roots in her own reckless behaviour on that occasion.

As she looked away from Ian, fixing her gaze on some point beyond him, she was astonished when Matthew moved towards her, almost coming to stand between Ian and herself, as though he sensed what she was feeling and wanted to reassure her, to protect her…

She was fantasising again, she derided herself, allowing emotions she had no right to feel take hold of her.

The sharp intensity of her awareness of Matt confused and alarmed her. When she moved away, instinctively trying to distance herself not just physically from him, but mentally from her own emotional reaction to him, he turned his head and looked at her.

It was only a brief glance—not a glance which she would ever have described as sexual or intimidating—and yet oddly it made her feel very much aware of herself as a woman and of him as a man.

This was getting ridiculous, she told herself shakily as she deliberately broke eye-contact with him. She was letting the past influence and overwhelm her judgement.

Matthew was speaking to Ian Jackson, telling him coolly and clinically about the complaints he had received.

Truculently Ian started to defend himself, his defence carrying veiled references to his influence over the men and the fact that certain 'perks' were a time-honoured tradition of the job.

Matt refused to give way, and Nicola could only admire the firmness with which he handled the situation.

When they eventually left the site, the foreman had been left in no doubt as to who was now in charge of the company, and of the manner in which Matt expected his employees to carry out their work.

On their way back to the Land Rover they had to walk past several of the men. Instinctively Nicola made a small detour to avoid coming too physically close to them.

It was only when she had circumvented them that she realised that Matt was watching her rather oddly. She could feel herself flushing.

It was an ingrained habit now, this need she had to keep as much physical distance between herself and the male sex—but not because she feared she might be approached or attacked. No, the reason for her behaviour had its roots in the night she met Matthew and the self-disgust which had been born in her then...a disgust which had been reinforced by Jonathon's sneeringly derogatory comments to her afterwards. She had told herself then that never, ever again would she give any man any reason to believe that she was encouraging him to think of her as sexually available.

She looked away from Matt now, her heart hammering with a mixture of fear and awareness.

She had seen the curiosity in his eyes, the thoughtfulness...the way he watched her wary, slightly uncoordinated movements, her tension as she hurried past the group of watching men.

By the time they reached the Land Rover her nervousness had increased. Not caring how inelegant she might look, she scrambled up into the passenger seat and sat tensely there as Matt climbed much more easily in beside her.

They were halfway back to the office when Matt said quietly, 'If any of the male members of the company are guilty of harassing female staff I should like to know about it. Not only because I disapprove on principle of men subjecting women to embarrassing and sometimes intimidating overtures they don't want, but also because there could be a very real threat of us losing business through such an attitude.'

Nicola bit her lip and gripped her hands together, shaking her head, knowing that, apart from the foreman, all the other men, while sometimes teasing the female employees, were not aggressive or unpleasant in their manner, and she certainly could not imply that they were just to save herself embarrassment.

'They…the men are all very pleasant,' she told him huskily.

There was a small pause, and then he enquired drily, 'Does that include Jackson?'

When she turned her head he was looking at her, a searching, intense look, which, if the past hadn't lain so painfully on her conscience, would have made her feel that there was nothing, no matter how personal, which she could not confide to him. A feeling of deep and intense sadness rolled through her, like grey clouds obscuring the sun, sending her spirits plummeting downwards.

'Ian isn't one of my favourite people,' she agreed, adding quickly, 'but the other men—'

Matt didn't allow her to finish.

'That kind of attitude from one man, especially one in the position which he holds, can all too easily influence the others, and I won't have it. As I said, it could affect us adversely where business is concerned. More and more women these days are making the decisions about extensions and so on to their homes, more and more women are single parents. When they have building work done they don't want to have to deal with someone like Jackson and, let's face it, when he and the men are on site they are virtually the only representatives of the company that our customers see.'

'The men respect him,' Nicola pointed out. 'He won't be easy to replace.'

'Not locally, perhaps, but I could always put someone in charge temporarily transferring them from one of my other concerns. However, it needn't come to that—if he alters his attitude...'

Privately Nicola suspected that the foreman would do no such thing. He was an arrogant man, used to dominating those around him, a man who depended on his swaggering, macho image. She sighed a little, mentally contrasting him with Matt, who was so very, very male, but in a totally different way. And yet that first time they had met...

Her forehead crinkled with confusion. *Then* he had seemed very much in the same macho mould as the foreman; *then* he had treated her with a careless disregard which, no matter how well-deserved, had left her sick with self-disgust. It was very hard to reconcile that man with the one seated next to her now.

Eight years is a long time, she reminded herself, and in those eight years social values had changed so much that it was perhaps only natural that human perceptions and reactions should change with them.

It surprised her how much she was enjoying working with Matt, but she was still haunted by the fear that something might happen and that he might look at her and realise...recognise her... and that then everything she had worked for— all the time and effort she had put into ensuring that never, ever again would she suffer the humiliation and trauma she had suffered when she'd woken up that morning in his bed—would be destroyed.

When he stopped the Land Rover in the yard he said easily, but very firmly, 'Stay there.'

Weakly Nicola did so, trembling a little as he came round to her side of the vehicle, opened the door, and reached in to help her out. She couldn't help flinching a little when he touched her. Just for a moment he tensed as though he had felt her physical reaction to him, but then he was helping her calmly and clinically from the Land Rover, quickly removing his hands from her waist once her feet could touch the ground.

'I understand that you have a steady boyfriend.'

The comment seemed to ricochet around inside her. Who on earth had told him about Gordon? And why? she wondered feverishly while she responded with a jerky, 'Er—yes...'

He gave her a sombre look that somehow seemed to hold a touch of loneliness, and then, astoundingly, told her flatly, 'He's a very fortunate man.'

As he turned on his heel and walked towards the office entrance, Nicola was left staring after him, feeling as though the ground was actually rocking precariously beneath her.

Had he really been trying to imply that he *envied* Gordon? Impossible, surely. If he wanted a woman in his life, there couldn't possibly be any shortage of candidates to fill that role.

To imply that he wanted *her*...

A tiny cold shiver of fear touched her spine.

What if it was all just a game? What if he was just playing with her, cruelly letting her believe that he didn't remember her, when in fact...? She gave another shiver, a deeper one this time. No. She was letting her fear get out of control. Why on earth would he want to behave in such a way? But to suggest that he found her attractive...that he envied Gordon...

Over the years there had been men who had wanted to get to know her better, but she had always frozen them off, afraid of the problems that intimacy with them might bring. With Gordon she was safe. Neither of them wanted anything more from their relationship than they already had. Gordon's life was dominated by his mother, a domination which, Nicola suspected, had resulted in an almost complete repression of his sexuality, while her life was dominated by her guilt and anguish over the past, which just as effectively repressed hers. If she allowed herself to fall in love with a man, eventually there would come a time when she would have to tell him about her past...to explain...because she was the type of woman who would want to be open and honest with someone she loved, but in doing so she would have to run the risk of them turning from her with the same contempt and disgust Jonathon had exhibited, and that was something she knew she could not endure. Better not to take the risk in the first place.

It terrified her to acknowledge that Matthew was a man whom she could quite easily have fallen in love with if the past hadn't stood between them. And what terrified her even more was the extent of her physical awareness of him.

All those years ago all her awareness, her attention, her emotions had been focused on Jonathon, but now she was wondering sickly if, beneath those emotions, some part of her had responded to Matt on a far deeper and more hidden level so that, even if she was not aware of it, she had been attracted to him...had been responsive to him...

Very slowly she followed him into the offices, telling herself that, once the new manager was installed and Matt was an infrequent visitor, she would be able to regain control of her life and her emotions, and in the meantime she would have to learn to live with the turbulence of what she was feeling.

ON FRIDAY she left home a little earlier than usual so that she could drop her car off at the garage.

One of the mechanics then drove her to work, giving her slender figure an admiring glance as she sat beside him.

Repressing an urge to tug down the skirt of her suit, Nicola feigned interest in something in the street outside the car, thankful when the mechanic finally took the hint and concentrated on driving the car rather than on trying to make conversation with her.

Evie arrived ten minutes after Nicola, the eye-catching brilliance of her outfit making Nicola blink a little and grin at her as she came rushing in.

Everyone bar Alan had been warned about the lunchtime gathering. Matt had undertaken to get

Alan there on time, and Nicola had no doubt that he would do so.

While she was going through the post, three of the men came in to dismantle Alan's desk.

Matt had asked why Alan wasn't taking it with him, commenting on its age and value, and Nicola had explained the situation.

'Well, it's his decision, but it's one he could regret later. I think what we'll do is have it dismantled and put in storage just in case he does change his mind.'

His decision was so close to the one she had privately already made that Nicola found herself trembling a little with the shock of the emotion that ran through her. She already knew that the new manager was going to be supplied with an equally new office, plus some very sophisticated computer equipment, which she herself was going to have to learn to use. Matt's confidence in her ability to do so had certainly been morale-boosting, if a little unnerving.

At eleven o'clock, once the more urgent en-quiries had been dealt with, Nicola told Evie,

'I'm just going to slip over to the store, to see if everything's under control.'

'What time are the caterers due?' Evie asked her.

'Half-past eleven.'

If had been Matt who had suggested bringing in outside caterers, adding casually that of course he would pay for the food and the drink they would need.

She had obtained several sample menus at modest prices, and had been even more surprised when Matt had announced that what he had in mind was something a little bit more substantial and enticing.

The caterers arrived exactly on time, unloading their van with very professional speed and assurance.

Large trestle-tables had been set up in the storage bay, which had been cleaned out especially for the occasion. It was a warm day, and motes of dust from the timber which had been stored there hung on the air, turning gold in the sunshine, the clean smell of timber sharp and pungent.

The caterers all wore uniforms, the girls in blue and white striped summer dresses with butchers' aprons over the tops, the men in navy trousers and blue and white striped shirts.

Matt had wanted to keep the affair as informal as possible, and so the long trestle-tables had been set up against the walls of the building with just one small table on a makeshift raised dais from which Matt would give his speech and present Alan with their gift.

As she looked round, watching the ordered busyness of the caterers, Nicola wondered how Alan would feel. This would be a very traumatic day for him—the final severing of his connection with the company he had worked so hard to build up, the final realisation, perhaps, that his son was dead.

She walked to the door of the shed and stood by it, her head bowed, emotional tears stinging her eyes as she dwelt on Alan's pain.

'Nicola…are you all right?'

She hadn't seen Matt approach, hadn't even

realised he was here, and now, shocked by the unexpected sound of his voice, she lifted her head jerkily and found that he was within a couple of feet of her, his forehead creased with concern as he came towards her.

He was dressed casually in worn jeans and a denim shirt, which was rolled back to reveal his forearms.

A pang of unexpected sensation tore through Nicola, destroying her frail self-control and, shockingly, she was almost instantly transported back into the past, to the memory of the way he had leaned over her that morning, his body smelling of soap and cologne, his—

'Nicola?'

She trembled as she fought off the unwanted memory, not realising it was the sight of the tears in her eyes that were provoking his harshness until he demanded, 'You're crying. Has someone…?'

Crying… She focused on him and then shook her head, explaining huskily, 'No, there's nothing wrong. I was just thinking of Alan—of how *he* must feel today. Where is he?' she added anxiously. 'It isn't twelve yet, and—'

'I know. I've left him over at the Waddington site. I made the excuse that I had an appointment I had to get back for, and told him I'd collect him later. I'm just on my way home to get changed, but I thought I'd better call in here and check that you weren't having any problems.'

Originally Matt had been staying in the town's one hotel, but now he had rented a property several miles away.

'Are you sure you're OK?' he asked her quietly.

One of the caterers came towards the door, and instinctively Nicola moved out of her way. Matt moved with her, so that disconcertingly they were both standing in the shadows, the pool of darkness casting a circle of intimacy around them. He had put his arm out to guide her to one side as the girl had come past, and now his hand was resting on the wall behind her, reinforcing the atmosphere of intimacy.

'Yes, yes. I'm fine…'

Was she trembling outwardly as much as she was inside and, if so, was he aware of it? She felt dizzy, confused, unable to move or think, and far too intensely aware of him. She couldn't bear to meet his eyes, and instead stared straight ahead of her. Which was a mistake. Her eyes seemed to be on a level with the bare column of his throat. His skin was tanned and smooth. She wanted, she realised with horror, to reach out and touch it…to touch him! She swallowed quickly, wishing her head would stop pounding so fast. She could see Matt's chest falling and lifting with his breathing.

Once she had leaned against that chest, once those hands had circled her body, had touched and caressed it, had known it so intimately that—

'Nicola!'

The sudden harshness in his voice shocked

through her, bringing her back to reality. She tensed, stepping as far back from him as she could, her eyes widening in response to the unexpected sensation of the wall against her back.

'I—I must go…the caterers…'

She heard herself babbling nervously, anxiety and fear tightening her body and her voice. Skirting him as carefully as though any kind of physical contact with him would be lethal to her, she edged past him and hurried towards the door. Behind her she could sense that he was moving, following her. Her mouth had gone dry, her muscles ached with tension.

'No car today,' Matt commented as he followed her outside.

She was forced to stop and turn round.

'No,' she told him jerkily. 'It's being serviced; Gordon is picking me up after work.'

She flushed, biting down hard on her bottom lip. Why had she brought Gordon into the conversation, like a teenager trying to deter an unwanted admirer with the clumsy subterfuge of introducing an existing boyfriend?

And it wasn't even as though Matt had even tried to— Just because he had paid her one compliment, it didn't mean…

'I'd better go and get changed. I'll have Alan back here for twelve-thirty.'

Was she imagining things or had Matt's voice become harder, curter?

Later, in her office, she asked herself what it was she was really so afraid of… Matt obviously hadn't recognised her and, even in the unlikely event of his actually being attracted to her, he obviously wasn't the kind of man to persist once he knew a woman was involved with someone else. So why was she so afraid? Why did she turn into something resembling a lump of quivering jelly every time he came near her?

She already knew the answer, and it wasn't one she welcomed. She closed her eyes, a weakening flood of shame and anguish pouring through her. Matt had been her first lover, her only lover, even if she could remember nothing of that time. That must be why she was so physically responsive to him, so physically aware of him. Her body must at some deep, atavistic level still be somehow aware of that long-ago intimacy with his.

THREE HOURS LATER, surveying the laughing, chattering mass of people centred in the shed, she reflected that Matt's decision to insist on this party for Alan had been the right one.

Although at first he had seemed shocked, reluctant almost to allow himself to be drawn into the proceedings, Alan had quite obviously been touched by his employees' wish to mark his retirement. There had been tears in his eyes when he was presented with the engraved goblet, and she had felt her admiration for Matt increase when, during his short speech, he had made a grave reference to the reason why Alan had taken the decision to sell the business. Many men and some women, too, would have shirked mentioning such a sensitive subject, too embarrassed by the potential emotional danger of it, to risk referring to it.

As she watched her fellow employees, Nicola found herself wishing that Matt was different…less likeable, more the man she had initially assumed him to be when they had first met.

Watching him now with the knowledge behind her of all she had recently learnt about him, she found it almost impossible to believe that this was the same man who had so casually picked her up and had sex with her; but, as she had reflected earlier, eight years was a long time, and the social climate had changed a great deal in those eight years.

At four o'clock people started to disperse, and Alan himself left. At four-thirty the caterers returned to start clearing up; most of her fellow employees had already left, following the traditional early closing down of the building trade on a Friday afternoon.

Gordon normally left his office at five o'clock, so Nicola knew it would be approaching five-thirty before he arrived to pick her up.

She had checked with the garage and knew

that they didn't close until six, which allowed them a reasonable margin of time to get there and collect her car.

She hadn't seen Matt for some time, and had assumed that he, too, must have left, but when she walked into her office, intending to finish off some work she had started earlier, she was startled to discover that the communicating door between her office and the one which had been Alan's, and which Matt was now using, was open, and that Matt himself, his jacket off, and his shirt-sleeves rolled up, was seated behind the new desk, poring over a sheaf of papers.

He had obviously heard her come in, though, because he put them down and looked up at her.

'Boyfriend not arrived yet?'

She shook her head, and then said huskily, 'He won't be here until about five-thirty, so I thought I'd just clear up a couple of things.'

As she spoke Matt stood up and moved away from his desk, stretching his body as he did so. She could hear the faint crack of his bones and closed her eyes, hating the wave of heat that burned through her as she became aware of his body, of the bulk and strength of it, of its lean, taut maleness…of the scent of his skin…the heat of his body.

'I was just about to make myself a cup of coffee… Want one?'

Alan, for all his gentleness, all his formality, would never have made such an offer. Her mouth dropped a little, and Matt, obviously taking her silence for agreement, walked past her and into the outer office, casually plugging in the kettle.

Nicola went back to her own desk. It was uncomfortable, disconcerting, knowing that Matt was moving about behind her as he made their coffee. She tried to concentrate on what she was doing, but her awareness of him kept coming between her and her work.

Long before he had come to stand beside her and place the mug of coffee down beside her she had known he was walking towards her.

'Going somewhere nice tonight—you and the

boyfriend?' he asked her casually as he stood beside her.

She frowned, unable for the moment to remember just exactly *what* they were doing, and then she recalled that it was Gordon's mother's monthly Friday for bridge, which meant that Gordon would have to take her and then pick her up, which meant that they would not be going out.

For some reason she felt reluctant to explain this to Matt, and so she fibbed as airily as she could. 'No, not really. Just out for something to eat, I expect, and then...'

'Back to his place,' Matt supplied drily.

His assumption that she and Gordon were lovers made her face burn, although she knew it was a natural enough assumption. She wasn't a young girl, she and Gordon were in an established relationship.

'Gordon lives with his mother,' she told him stiffly.

There was a long pause, during which she

didn't look at him, but attempted instead to concentrate on what was in front of her. It was a hopeless task. She was so very aware of Matt standing beside her that there wasn't room in her consciousness for anything else.

When at last the tension in the silence was something she couldn't bear any longer, she asked him quickly, 'And you—are you going out tonight?'

Immediately she wished the question unasked. After all, what business of hers was it what he did in his private life? The thought that he might think she was asking out of a personal interest in that private life dismayed her.

'I'm going to see my parents. They live just outside Brighton. They moved there several years ago when my father retired, primarily because one of my sisters lives in that area and my parents wanted to be close to their grandchildren. My second sister and her husband live in Canada.

'Do you have any siblings?'

'No, I'm an only one...' She frowned as she

looked across the room at the wall-clock and saw that it was almost a quarter to six.

'Something wrong?' Matt asked her.

She shook her head, but obviously he wasn't convinced because he asked shrewdly, 'Boy-friend late?'

When her only response was to bite her lip, he said casually, 'You'd better give him a ring. Didn't you say he was taking you to collect your car?'

Tactfully he returned to his own office while she picked up the receiver and then telephoned the number of Gordon's office.

As she had half expected, no one answered.

She waited another five minutes, all the time anxiously aware that she was now going to be unable to reach the garage before it closed, and then rather grimly dialled Gordon's home tele-phone number.

He answered the telephone himself, his voice sharply defensive when she reminded him that he was supposed to have picked her up.

'Mother isn't very well,' he told her. 'I had to come home early from the office, and I just haven't been able to leave her. It's one of her bilious attacks, and you know how badly they affect her.'

Nicola certainly did. Gordon's mother's bilious attacks had been the cause of more outings being cancelled than she cared to remember.

'You might have rung me and let me know, Gordon,' she commented a little sharply. 'I'm not going to be able to get to the garage in time to collect my car now.'

'Well, you can collect it in the morning, can't you? I mean, you won't need it tonight, and your father can run you into town in the morning.'

'I still have to get home tonight,' Nicola reminded him crossly, trying not to react too angrily to his complete lack of regard for her and their arrangements.

'I'm sorry, Nicola,' he told her, sounding anything but. 'But with poor Mother feeling so very unwell…'

It was only by reminding herself that she was twenty-six and not sixteen that Nicola managed to refrain from slamming down the receiver on him.

She was just dialling the number of a local taxi firm when Matt emerged from his office.

'Something wrong?' he questioned her.

She put down the receiver and explained tersely, 'Gordon isn't going to be able to pick me up after all. I was just ringing for a taxi to take me home.'

'Don't bother,' Matt told her easily. 'I'll run you back.'

Immediately hot colour stormed her face. 'Oh, no. There's no need for that,' she began to object, worried that he might think she had been angling for the offer of a lift; but he brushed aside her protestations, telling her mildly,

'It really isn't any problem. I have to virtually go past your gate, anyway.'

Nicola gave him a startled look. She hadn't realised he even knew where she lived and, as though he were reading her mind, he informed her casually, 'Evie happened to mention where you live. Are you ready to go now or—?'

'Yes, I'm ready,' she confirmed.

As they were walking out to the Land Rover, he commented almost disapprovingly, 'It's a pity your boyfriend didn't think to ring you earlier, then you could have made other arrangements to collect your car.'

Immediately, and for no good reason that she could think of, Nicola discovered that she was lying to protect Gordon as she protested untruthfully, 'Oh, he did ring earlier to leave a message, but he couldn't get through...'

When she turned her head, driven by some impulse she couldn't control, she discovered that Matt had stopped walking, and that he was regarding her with a grim, almost bitter expression in his eyes.

'You're very loyal, aren't you, Nicola? I wonder if he is equally loyal to you.'

The gibe made her flush a little, partly because she knew just how luke-warm Gordon's feelings for her were, and partly because she felt that she herself was guilty of allowing Matt to think that her relationship with Gordon was far more emotionally intense than it actually was.

Reluctantly she followed Matt, who was standing waiting for her.

OF COURSE BOTH her parents would have to be in the front garden when Matt turned the Land Rover into the drive, and of course Matt would have to accept when her mother asked if he had time to join them for a cup of tea.

In the end he stayed for over an hour, and as far as Nicola was concerned it put the final, irritating thorn in her day when, after he had gone, her mother asked innocently,

'I thought that Gordon was picking you up and taking you to the garage? Not that I didn't enjoy meeting Matt. He's an extremely attractive and intelligent man—'

'Gordon's mother isn't well,' Nicola said shortly, valiantly trying to ignore the look in her mother's eyes.

Privately she suspected that Gordon was beginning to find their relationship as onerous as she did herself, and, if it weren't for Matt she knew now for sure that she would have been tempted to suggest to Gordon that they simply stopped seeing one another.

CHAPTER SIX

'IT'S tonight that you and Gordon are having dinner with Christine and Mike, isn't it?'

'Yes,' Nicola agreed in answer to her mother's question. She had been working with Matt for over a fortnight now, and the office work had settled into an efficient and orderly routine. She only wished it were equally easy to rule her chaotic emotions.

It was impossible now for her to deny to herself that Matt had a very powerful and disruptive effect upon her emotionally and physically, but just so long as she was the only person who knew that…just so long as she managed to conceal it from everyone else she might manage to make it safely through the next few weeks until the new manager was able to take over from Matt.

She was feeling increasingly out of charity with Gordon. He had broken several of their dates with a variety of weak excuses, and she had promised herself that if he dared to break tonight's then she was going to tell him that she no longer wanted to see him.

At half-past seven when the telephone rang and she answered it to learn from Gordon that he was not going to be able to join her that evening, she gritted her teeth and told him acidly that in that case she saw no point in their seeing one another again at all.

Although he protested a little, she could tell that really he was relieved by her decision.

'Was that Gordon?' her mother enquired, when she replaced the receiver.

'Yes,' Nicola told her, adding emotionlessly, 'He can't make it tonight. His mother isn't well again. I've told him that I don't think there's any point in our continuing to see one another—at least not on a one-to-one basis.'

It was her mother's softly commiserating,

'Oh, darling, I'm so sorry,' that made her eyes sting a little.

'You needn't be. It isn't like that,' she assured her. 'After all, it was hardly the relationship of the century. I expect I shall miss him, but I'm not exactly heartbroken.'

'Well, he *is* rather dull, and I must admit I could never understand what you saw in him. I'm afraid dull, worthy men have never really appealed to me. Now *Matt*, for instance…'

Nicola felt her heart jerk as though it were held on strings. Her voice was sharper than she realised when she said fiercely, 'Matt is my *boss*, Mum, nothing more. He won't be here for much longer, anyway, and—'

Realising that she was perhaps over-protesting, she stopped speaking. It was too late now to ring Christine and cancel, but fortunately she knew her friend well enough to know that she wouldn't mind her turning up on her own.

Christine had mentioned that she had invited some business acquaintances of Mike's, but that the dinner was an informal rather than a formal affair.

Nicola had been virtually ready when Gordon telephoned. Her dress wasn't new, being a simple affair in navy silk which she had bought the previous summer. It had a neat round neckline and long sleeves, and was, so she thought, eminently suitable for a woman who preferred not to catch the male eye.

What she did not realise was that the softness of the silk married to the willow slimness of her figure gave her dress an understated sensuality that was far, far more enticing than something more figure-hugging and eye-catching would have been. It was the sort of dress that made a man look once and then look again, his attention drawn by the feminine movement of her body beneath its demure sheath of silk.

With it she was wearing sheer navy tights and plain navy pumps. Some spirit of defiance made her add a slightly darker lip-gloss than normal, although once it was on she was tempted to rub it off as she unwillingly remembered the scarlet lipstick she had once worn. As she hesitated, she realised that if she delayed much longer she might not be the first to arrive, which would mean that she wouldn't have an opportunity to explain what had happened with Gordon to her friend in private.

When Christine opened the door to her half an hour later, as Nicola had known she would, she raised her eyebrows and asked, 'Where's Gordon?'

'Not coming,' Nicola told her grimly, and went on to relay recent events.

'Well, it's about time you got rid of him,' Christine told her forthrightly.

'I don't think I so much got rid of him, as let him off the hook and put him out of his misery,' Nicola told her drily, adding, 'Look, if my being here on my own is going to mess up your numbers—'

'Don't be an idiot. As a matter of fact, it will actually even them out. Mike invited a business associate, who doesn't have a wife or, apparently, a current girlfriend…'

When she saw Nicola's face she laughed. 'Don't worry. I'm not trying to matchmake. I haven't even met him yet.'

She went on to explain that the other two guests were also business associates of her husband's. Nicola knew them vaguely, as they had recently moved into the area.

'Anything I can do to help?' she offered.

'Go upstairs and read Peter a story. He knows you're coming and he's been pestering me all day about it. Now there's a man for you…if you can wait twenty odd years for him to grow up,' she teased, while Nicola pulled a face at her before heading for the stairs.

Half an hour later, when she heard male feet coming upstairs and stopping just inside the bedroom door, she said softly without turning her head, 'Hello, Mike. He's just dropped off…'

Only when she turned her head to smile at her friend's husband she discovered that it wasn't Mike who was standing there, but Matt.

Her heart seemed to do a triple somersault

before starting to bounce erratically around inside her chest. Although she automatically started to stand up, the shock of seeing Matt made her sit down again and stare at him in mute disbelief.

'Christine sent me up to tell you that she's just about to serve dinner,' he told her softly, pitching his voice so that it didn't disturb the little boy sleeping in his bed.

Matt, here? It seemed impossible, like some kind of waking dream. She felt as though if she shook her head she would somehow be able to make him disappear, but when she did so, to her consternation, he remained stubbornly exactly where he was, waiting for her…watching her.

Uncertainly she got to her feet, unaware of how many betraying emotions were reflected in her eyes as she walked tensely towards the door.

Why hadn't Christine warned her that Matt would be here? Probably because her friend was scatty enough not to have made the connection between Mike's new client and her own new boss, Nicola recognised numbly as she walked downstairs.

In a daze she walked into the dining-room and was introduced to the other couple. The wife, Lucinda, ignored Nicola completely, focusing all her attention on Matt—in a way that made Nicola's heart somersault again, but this time in a very different way.

She was an enviably tall redhead with sharp green eyes and a full but somehow predatory mouth. She was wearing a scarlet silk dress which ought to have clashed with her hair but which somehow did not, its neckline displaying a generous amount of cleavage.

It was plain that her husband doted on her, and it was also equally plain as the meal progressed that she was the kind of woman who had very little time for her own sex. All her attention and her conversation was conferred on Matt and, as she struggled to get something more out of her husband than a laconic 'Yes' or 'No' in response to her questions, Nicola tried to tell herself that it was absolutely no concern of hers if Lucinda flirted with Matt, nor if he chose to respond.

It wasn't until they had reached the pudding stage of the meal that she finally admitted to herself that the feeling boiling up inside her, as she tried not to listen to Lucinda's very obvious flirtation with Matt, was one of jealous resentment.

Pushing away her pudding barely touched, she raised her head to discover very disconcertingly that Matt was looking at her.

She could feel the hot tide of colour burning slowly up her body as she wondered how long she had been the focus of his attention and if he could possibly have recognised what she was feeling, while praying that he hadn't.

It wasn't until after the meal was over that she realised how quiet and engrossed she must have been, because Christine asked her when she was helping her to clear the table, 'Are you OK? You didn't seem too upset earlier when you told me about Gordon, but…'

Numbly Nicola shook her head, unable to

explain even to one of her closest friends what she was really feeling.

'Look, I know I've said some pretty callous things about him…and I still don't think that he was the right one for you…but if you want to talk about it, or just have a damn good cry…'

Again Nicola shook her head, wondering half hysterically what on earth Chris would say if she admitted that she had barely given Gordon a thought all evening, and that instead it was Matt who was occupying not just her thoughts but her emotions as well.

Giving her a quick, concerned look, Christine turned round and then exclaimed warmly, 'Matt, you shouldn't have bothered, but thanks anyway…' as she went to take from him the empty dishes he had carried through to the kitchen.

Nicola almost dropped the things she was holding. She had had no idea that Matt was there. Her heart started thumping frantically. She closed her eyes, visualising what could have happened if she had confided in Christine and he had overheard.

What was there to confide anyway—that once long ago she had spent the night with him, and had been too drunk to have any recollection of what had happened? That he had casually informed her that they had been lovers, and that because of the public way she had left the party with him she had been taunted with her lack of morals and her sexual availability? That because of that she had come running home sick at heart and distraught? That because of that she had shunned all further sexual contact with men, sickened by her own behaviour and knowing that any decent, worthwhile man would feel the same way?

How could she tell Chris that after that she was now discovering a very different Matt Hunt from the one she remembered, and that, even worse, she was finding herself becoming more and more emotionally vulnerable and drawn to him…that she was like a cold and hungry creature fascinated by fire and warmth, and drawn desperately into seeking it…circling it with hunger and fear, wanting its warmth and yet terrified of it at the same time?

She closed her eyes, feeling the tension draining her energy.

What was she trying to tell herself—that she was falling in love with Matthew Hunt? She made a small, derisory sound under her breath, causing both Matt and Chris to look at her.

Skirting past Matt, she hurried back to the dining-room, determinedly busying herself collecting more empty plates, while she tried frantically to deny the knowledge her own brain was giving her.

The rest of the evening was a form of purgatory. Not only had she to contend with the knowledge that no matter what the reason, and no matter how dangerous and self-destructive it was, she was quite definitely emotionally responsive to Matt in a way which had previously been totally outside her experience. She had thought once that she was in love with Jonathon, but then she had been a child, now she was a woman. An adult—it was like comparing the flicker of a torchlight with the full power of the sun. And it wasn't just that she was emotionally responsive to Matt... Physically, she— She flinched inwardly, knowing that she was so aware of him that even without turning her head she knew exactly where he was in the room... that without looking at him she could conjure up the sensations that invaded and disturbed her whenever he came close to her.

She told herself fiercely that she was glad that Lucinda was monopolising him, because that way *she* was in no danger of making a fool of herself by... By what? By betraying to him the effect he was having on her?

If Chris hadn't been one of her oldest friends, she would have made some excuse and left early. But Nicola was already bitterly aware of the fact that Chris was concerned about her and errone-ously believed that she was upset about the ending of her relationship with Gordon. If she left early, Chris was bound to think that it was because of Gordon and, no matter how much she denied it, Chris wouldn't believe her unless she told her the truth.

The temptation to do just that astounded her. She wanted, she realised miserably, to talk about Matt, as though somehow just by speaking his name she would be easing the growing ache inside herself. Then the awareness of how quickly she had travelled down a very, very dangerous road made her feel slightly sick. She wanted to go home…to be alone…to try to find some way of controlling what was happening to her.

Lucinda's voice had a certain shrill metallic quality to it, and now it intruded into her silence, causing her to turn her head. Lucinda was standing with Matt, her hand on his arm while she pouted up at him. Her body was almost, but not quite, resting against his, the soft thrust of her breasts clearly discernible. Standing so close to her, Matt could not help but breathe in her perfume and be aware of her body.

The sick helplessness that clawed at her own stomach appalled Nicola. She discovered that she was actually physically shaking in reaction, not just to her jealousy but also to her own disgust at it.

When she heard Frank Barrett announcing that it was time he and Lucinda left, since they had the baby-sitter to run home, the relief that flowed through her was so total and immediate that it made her feel physically weak—not because their departure would remove Lucinda from Matt's presence, but because it meant that she herself could also leave.

She waited for an unbearable ten minutes after the Barretts had gone before announcing that she too must leave. Chris tried to persuade her to stay, watching her worriedly as she half whispered, 'If you want to talk about…things…'

She shook her head in denial, fibbing uncomfortably, 'I'm just a bit tired.'

Mike, who had caught what she'd said, grinned at her, putting a friendly arm around her shoulders as he teased, 'Not because this new boss of yours is working you too hard, I hope?'

Nicola hoped she sounded far more natural to their ears than she did to her own as she forced herself to smile and laugh back.

'Gordon couldn't make it, then?' Mike added conversationally, plainly not yet aware of what had happened.

Out of the corner of her eye Nicola saw Chris made a small moue of dismay and shake her head warningly at her husband.

'His mother isn't well,' Nicola responded shortly. With Matt standing there she wasn't about to explain to Mike that there wasn't any 'her and Gordon' any more.

The entire evening had been a strain on her, which, coupled with everything else that had happened over the last few weeks, was making her feel as though her whole life was somehow slipping out of her control, Nicola acknowledged as she unlocked the door of her car and got inside.

Chris and Mike lived on the other side of the

town from her parents, but she was less than halfway home when she suddenly discovered that she was trembling so violently that she could barely control the car.

Immediately she pulled off the road into a convenient layby, quickly switching off the engine.

Everything around her had become frighteningly blurred, but it wasn't until she raised her hand to her face that she discovered that she was actually crying.

Her chest felt tight with pain and she couldn't stop trembling. She leaned forward, closing her eyes, resting her head on the steering-wheel, too overwhelmed by what was happening to her to do anything else.

It took the sudden realisation that someone was opening her car door to jerk her back to real awareness of the fact that she was parked on a very lonely stretch of road, that it was dark and well past midnight, and that she was completely on her own.

However, no sooner had a series of panicky

thoughts started to flood her mind than she realised that the person opening the door was Matt.

'I saw you'd stopped and thought you might be having car trouble,' he explained tersely.

It was too late to make any attempt to hide her tears from him. The swiftly comprehensive glance he had given her in the light flooding the car as he'd opened the door must have revealed her tear-stained face quite clearly.

'The car's fine, thanks,' she told him.

'It's him, isn't it—the boyfriend?' he demanded almost roughly. 'I heard you telling Christine that it was all over between you.'

He stood up, closing her driver's door before she could say anything.

For a few seconds she thought he had gone, and then she realised he had simply walked around the car and was now opening the passenger door and getting in.

While she stared at him, torn between the agonising pleasure of having him there and the realisation of how dangerous to her this kind of intimacy was, she heard him saying huskily, 'I know you'll have heard this already, but he really isn't worth it. The man must be a fool if he doesn't realise…'

He thought she was crying because of *Gordon*. Automatically Nicola turned to him to deny it, but he was sitting far too close to her in the small confines of her compact car and, as she turned her head, he raised his hand, his fingers warm and hard as they slid against her face, his thumb brushing away the damp traces of her tears.

'He isn't worth it,' he told her again.

She started to tremble, heat flooding her. Her skin was burning where he was touching it. She had a wild impulse to turn her head and let her lips explore the hand that cupped her face. She trembled again.

'Nicki, don't…'

She had no awareness of either of them moving, but one or both of them must have done because suddenly there was no distance between them at all. Matt's free arm was holding her against him, while his hand slid into her hair, the touch of his fingers against her scalp almost— almost tender, she recognised dazedly.

She looked up at him, mutely searching his face, not really understanding what was motivating his intimacy with, and concern for, her.

Shadows cloaked his features. All she could see was the dark glitter of his eyes, the male outline of his mouth as he turned his head towards her.

Her heart jerked painfully inside her chest. She discovered that, having focused on his mouth, she could not bring herself to look away.

Her throat had gone dry, her lungs seemed incapable of drawing in enough air, her lips parted, a million tiny, aching pulses beating through her body.

'Nicki…'

His voice was rough, its timbre making her shiver as though he had actually touched her skin, caressing its most sensitive points.

When his lips first touched hers, it was no more

than a whisper of sensation, a soft brushing of flesh on flesh, but it sensitised her so much that she trembled bodily.

Immediately Matt made a soft sound of reassurance against her mouth. His tongue stroked her lips, and instinctively she felt herself trying to get even closer to him. Her arms were wrapped around him, although she had no real awareness of how they had got there.

The slow stroke of his tongue against her lips was dangerously erotic, making her ache for something more intimate. Her muscles clenched fiercely as her senses reacted to her mind's imagery of how that yearned-for intimacy would make her feel.

Matt wasn't wearing a jacket, and beneath her fingertips she could feel the hard play of his muscles.

Overwhelmed by her own physical responsiveness to him, she caressed his back and then his shoulders, mindlessly letting her emotions and desires take control of her.

This must be something she had done before, surely, otherwise how would her hands, her entire body, yearn for such intimacy?

When Matt's mouth left hers to caress her throat she made a small, keening sound of distress, her body trembling with urgency, an ache of need coiling tautly through her.

She must have said his name, although she had no knowledge of having done so, because almost immediately his mouth returned to hers and he was kissing her not as he had done before— gently and exploratively—but with an intimacy that made her body arch and her mouth open in eager invitation.

She felt the shudder that convulsed him, her own body registering it and reacting in an aftershock of small tremors. Her breasts were pressed hard against his body and had started to ache almost unbearably, not from the pressure of their embrace but from a far more private, primitive and sensual cause.

She wanted his hands on her body, she recognised, and not just his hands… She closed her eyes, shivering, drenched by the hot tide of need that rocked through her.

Outside, beyond the intimate darkness of the car, a horn blared, tyres squealing in protest as one car overtook another, the noise shocking her into abruptly focusing on what she was doing.

As he felt her tense, Matt let her go, his voice low and slightly rough as he apologised.

'I'm sorry. I never meant…I didn't intend…'

This time, the burning sensation under her skin was caused not by desire but by embarrassment, the embarrassment of knowing what Matt was telling her.

'Look, why don't you leave your car here and let me drive you home?' he continued. 'You're upset and—'

'I'm perfectly capable of driving,' she told him brittly. She wasn't and she knew it, but she felt as though if she had to spend any more time with him she would shatter like a piece of over-stressed glass.

She still wasn't sure quite what had happened to her, or how what she knew Matt had only intended as a gesture of comfort had turned into the fiercely burning physical desire she had experienced.

If that was how she had behaved that night, no wonder he had looked so—so smug and self-satisfied in the morning, she thought sickly.

She closed her eyes briefly against the hot burn of fresh tears and said thickly, 'Please, go…I want to get home…'

She tensed as she felt him hesitate, knowing that if he argued with her now she would probably break down completely.

'Go, Matt,' she demanded. 'Please…'

To her relief he opened the car door and made to get out, pausing to tell her, 'I still don't think you're in any fit state to drive, so I'll follow you to make sure you get home safely. No arguments,' he added curtly. 'Otherwise, I'll carry you out of this damn thing by force if necessary…'

Silently Nicola watched him go, suppressing the temptation to race off into the night before he could return to his own car, knowing that he'd been quite right when he'd said she wasn't really fit to drive.

Luckily the roads were quiet but, despite the fact that she applied all her concentration to the task of driving, she was very conscious of the fact that physically she felt oddly weak, and that her mind kept straying, drawn dangerously into a whirlpool of thoughts and fears which had nothing to do with what she was doing and everything to do with what had happened with Matt.

When she turned into her parents' drive, she glanced in her driving-mirror and saw that Matt's car was parked at the end of the drive.

He had been behind her all the way home, monitoring what she was doing, watching over her. What had motivated him to do that? Guilt, because he felt responsible for her distraught state? But why should he feel guilty when she had been the one...?

She shuddered as she stopped the car, remembering how she had moaned beneath his mouth in aching frustration, wanting more…wanting him… Her skin flushed and she was glad that there was no one to see her, to witness her shame and anguish.

That Matt had never intended to do more than offer her a comforting male shoulder to cry on she already knew. Even that first tentative pressure of his mouth on hers had been comforting rather than arousing.

As she went inside, she found herself almost wishing that he had remembered her at first sight. Then, she had no doubt that he would have avoided her like the plague, then there would have been no intimacy between them to taunt and disturb her. Then he would have remembered how she had reacted to him before, even if she could not, and he would have acted accordingly.

Her first initial fear on recognising him—that he would remember her and cause her humiliation and embarrassment by doing so, by making her behaviour public—no longer existed. He was simply not that kind of man. Witness his behaviour towards her tonight… His kindness. His concern.

He had even apologised for what had happened when both of them knew that the real blame lay with her.

Ironically, once she was alone and free to cry, she discovered that she no longer had any real desire to do so. Neither, it seemed, was she going to be able to get much sleep, because every time she closed her eyes she was tormented by far too vivid memories of how she had felt when Matt had kissed and held her.

Matthew Hunt… *Why* was she so susceptible to him? Was it because of the past? As she curled her body into a small, tight ball of distress, she tried to convince herself that, once Matt had left the area, once he was only someone who visited the company at rare intervals, she would soon overcome her present feelings—that, starved of the object of their desire, her emotions would soon be back under her control. And just as long as Matt thought, as he obviously did think, that she loved Gordon, she would be reasonably safe from the humiliation of his realising how she felt about him.

A tiny, bitter smile curved her mouth. How ironic of fate to send him back into her life like this… How ironic and cruel. The sensuality which she had denied she possessed for all these years had, with Matt's arrival, suddenly burst into eager life, tormenting her with desires and needs with which she was wholly unfamiliar. Even now, hours later, the mere memory of his lips touching hers had the power to make her whole body go taut with aching heat. She even found herself wishing that she could remember that night she had spent with him so that she could…

So that she could what? Relive it, if only mentally? Miserably she closed her eyes and willed herself to at least try to go to sleep.

CHAPTER SEVEN

'NICOLA, meet Tim Ford.'

'A rather delayed meeting, I'm afraid,' Tim commented as he and Nicola shook hands.

They were in Nicola's office, where she had arrived ten minutes earlier to discover that Matt was already there and that their new manager was with him, having been able to return to work a little earlier than had originally been anticipated.

Trying to ignore the shock of anguish that had hit her with the realisation that her daily contact with Matt would soon be a thing of the past, Nicola reminded herself that if she had any sense she would be feeling relieved that Tim Ford had arrived.

Since the night he had followed her home from

the dinner party, she had been so acutely aware of Matt that working with him had become an almost unbearable strain.

She was losing weight and growing tense and, even though she knew that her parents and her friends were concerned about her and had erroneously put the change in her down to her break-up with Gordon, she couldn't bring herself to admit the truth to any of them.

It had taken her long enough to admit it to herself. She was in love with Matt.

She looked at him now, a quick, surreptitious glance under cover of the conversation he was having.

During office hours, Matt had made no reference whatsoever to what had happened between them, but on the day following the dinner party he had called round totally unexpectedly to see her. She had been in the garden, picking some peas for lunch, her hair scraped back off her face, and dressed in a pair of tatty jeans and an equally old T-shirt.

His grave apology for what had happened had left her tonguetied with guilt and shame, wanting to tell him that she was equally responsible, but unable to find the words to do so.

He wanted her to know, he had told her, that she need have no fear of suffering the embarrassment of any kind of sexual harassment from him; he knew she loved Gordon; they were both adults, both aware that the most innocuous of events, when coloured by very powerful emotions, could result in things happening which had never been intended to happen.

What he was trying to tell her was that he had never intended to do anything more than ensure that she was all right. She already knew that, and his apology had made her feel even worse than she had done before, especially when she had happened to look up at him and all too betrayingly remembered what it had felt like to be held in his arms, to have his mouth caressing hers.

When he'd suggested that both of them put the

entire incident out of their minds, she'd been only too willing to agree.

She realised that Tim Ford was speaking to her, and quickly dragged her attention back to focus on what he was saying.

He was a pleasant-looking man in his early thirties, whom, she had learned, was unmarried, and who had worked for Matt for several years.

His leg was still in plaster from the accident which had immobilised him and caused the delay in his taking over from Alan.

'Site visits are going to be tricky for a while,' he told Nicola ruefully while Matt was taking a phone call.

He then went on to ask her how she was liking the new computer systems they were having installed, and whether she had found them to be of any benefit.

Within half an hour of meeting him, Nicola knew she could work in harmony with him, probably more efficiently than she could work for Matt, with whom she was never free of the

tensions caused by her awareness of him as
a man.

Matt had finished his call and, when she
glanced across at him, unable to resist the temptation of looking at him, she saw that he was regarding them with a slight frown. Her own
muscles tensed in response. Had she done something wrong, irritated him in some way?

His, 'If you've got a moment, Tim, there are a
few things I'd like to run through with you,' was
curt and, as Tim walked towards the open door
between the two offices, Nicola heard Matt
adding even more curtly to her,

'I'm sure you've got things to do, Nicola, so
we won't take up any more of your time.'

His formal 'Nicola,' when for days he had been
referring to her as Nicki, hurt, as did the very
cold and obvious way he was making it clear that
he didn't want her to join them.

Stupid of her to take it so personally, she told
herself ten minutes later, when the door was very
firmly closed between their offices, and she was

seated at her own desk, working busily. And that was the trouble. She had become far, far too personally involved with Matt, with her own feelings for him…feelings which she knew quite well he could never reciprocate. And even if he did…what would happen when she had to explain…tell him? It went against everything she believed in most strongly to keep the truth from him. It would have been bad enough to have to tell him what had happened had the man concerned been someone else, but when that man was Matt himself…

Why was she worrying so much about something that was never going to happen? she asked herself miserably half an hour later. As far as Matt was concerned, she was still in love with Gordon and, for the sake of her own pride and self-respect, it was far, far better that he continued to think so.

When the inner office door opened, and Matt and Tim walked out, Matt told her briefly, 'We're just off to lunch now, Nicola. We shouldn't be too long—'

Tim, who was standing behind him, frowned a little and interrupted, 'Oh, but I thought that Nicola was coming with us…'

'I'm sure she's got far more important things to do with her lunch-hour,' Matt contradicted him flatly—so flatly that Nicola bent her head over the papers on her desk, not wanting either man to see the hurt that Matt's coolness was causing her.

Ten minutes later, acknowledging that, while she really didn't feel like anything to eat, some food would probably do her good, she collected her jacket and left the office.

It was only a short walk into the small town's centre. Wednesday was market day and the town was busy, but the waitress still managed to find a small table for Nicola in the window of her favourite wine-bar, where she could watch the people coming and going outside.

She was just about to start her meal when Christine walked in and saw her.

'Nicki! I thought I might find you in here,' she

greeted her enthusiastically as she sat down, eyeing Nicola's plate of pasta enviously as she commented ruefully, 'Lucky you, you can eat what you like. I'm beginning to look like a house, and now that I'm pregnant again…'

She laughed as Nicola congratulated her, admitting that both she and Mike were thrilled about the new baby.

'You should get married and have one yourself,' Christine teased her, biting her lip in mortification as she apologised contritely. 'Oh, Nicki, I'm so sorry. That was tactless of me when you and Gordon…'

'I'm not bothered about Gordon,' Nicola told her quietly. 'In fact—well, let's just say it was probably the best thing for both of us. After all, we were never anything more than friends, and not even particularly good friends… Our relationship was a convenience that suited us both at the time.'

'Then why are you looking as though the world's suddenly caved in on top of you?' Christine demanded, watching her, adding, 'And don't try denying that something's wrong, Nicki. You've lost weight, you hardly ever seem to smile these days… In fact, you're exhibiting all the classic signs of unrequited love.'

She stopped and bit her lip again, and then said softly, 'Oh, Nicki, it isn't Gordon at all, is it? It's Matthew Hunt.'

Nicola pushed her food away almost un-touched, and said bitterly, 'It's the classic thing, isn't it—the dull, plain secretary falling for her handsome, sexy boss…?'

'No one would ever describe you as dull or plain,' Christine objected, adding thoughtfully, 'Is it really unrequited, Nicki? I mean, I couldn't help noticing at our dinner party that he seemed to want to be with you.'

'I think that was just so that he could evade Lucinda's clutches,' Nicola told her lightly. 'I don't want to discuss it if you don't mind, Chris. It's just one of those things, and I'm bound to get over it… Just as long as too many people don't make the same lightning deductions you've just made. I hadn't realised I was being so obvious…'

'You aren't,' Christine assured her. 'I just happen to know you very well, that's all.'

'Well, I'd certainly rather people thought I was heartbroken over Gordon than know the truth. Matt's leaving the area soon. The new manager arrived today and, once he's settled in, Matt will be little more than a casual visitor.'

'Leaving, is he?' Christine asked in surprise. 'Well, he hasn't said anything to Mike about terminating his lease of the house. In fact, I thought Mike said he wanted to extend it.'

Nicola shrugged.

'I wouldn't know. Maybe he's keeping it on for Tim Ford, that's the new man. After all, rented property isn't easy to come by round here.' She paused, toying worriedly with her uneaten food, and then, keeping her head bent, asked in a low voice, 'You won't say anything about—about this…even to Mike, will you, Chris?'

Tears stung her eyes when Christine put her

hand over hers and assured her firmly, 'Trust me, Nicki. I can well remember how I felt when I first fell in love with Mike, and I thought he wasn't interested. I think I'd have died then if I'd thought that someone might inadvertently have told him that I loved him. I shan't mention it to anyone—and that includes Mike. It may not be as bad as you think, you know,' she added softly. 'I couldn't help noticing how attentive he was to you over dinner.'

'He was just being polite,' Nicola told her shortly. She didn't want anyone trying to raise her hopes, encouraging her to believe in something she already knew didn't exist, and, besides, not even Chris knew the whole story. That chapter of her life, the time she had spent in the city, was something she had never discussed with anyone.

'I'd better go back,' she told Christine, pushing away her plate and standing up. 'I'm thrilled for you both about the baby.'

'Just as well, because we intend to ask you to

be godmother,' Chris told her with a grin but, as she watched her friend walk away, her smile was replaced by a small, anxious frown. Poor Nicki; she wished there was something she could do to help her.

WITH TIM FORD'S arrival, Nicola noticed a new distance between herself and Matt. It was perhaps only natural that he should take a back seat, allowing Tim to take over the reins of running the business, but still, it hurt unbearably when she turned to query something with him to be referred almost curtly to Tim.

And, when he had to speak with her, she found that he was standing almost feet away from her, whereas before she had often found him standing so close to her that their bodies had actually been touching. Many, many times she had had to resist the impulse to allow herself to lean into him, to savour the intimacy of even the briefest physical contact with him, even while she deplored her own lack of self-control.

Now there was no need for her to exercise any form of physical self-control; the distance Matt kept between them saw to that.

On his final morning in the office, Matt arrived late, and announced that he was leaving earlier than planned—at lunchtime.

He had, he announced, decided to take a few days off, which he explained he intended to spend with his parents.

'My sister and her family are over from Canada. I haven't really seen her since she got married two years ago.'

'Do you have many nieces and nephews?' Nicola found herself asking him a little enviously. She had always wished she had a larger family, brothers and sisters…and she envied Matt his married sisters and his extended family.

'Two nieces, three nephews and one "don't know" as yet,' he told her briefly, a warm smile touching his mouth.

That warm smile made Nicola's stomach

muscles quiver. She was, she discovered shockingly, almost ragingly jealous of his unknown family and the obvious love he had for them.

He had added that he would probably leave at about two o'clock and, even though she hated herself for doing so, Nicola discovered that she was surreptitiously shortening her own lunch-break so that she would be back in the office well before two, like a miser greedily hoarding every extra second of his presence.

Only when she walked into the yard, there was no sign of his now familiar car and, when she passed Tim in the foyer, he told her casually that Matt had already left.

She was glad she was standing in the shadows, instinctively turning her head away from him so that he wouldn't see her despair.

'I was wondering,' she heard him adding un-certainly, 'if you could give me a few tips on how to get involved in the local social life... I'm rather past the age for discos and the like, but not exactly old enough to join the pipe-and-slippers brigade… I don't play golf and—'

'I could introduce you to some people if you like,' Nicola offered instinctively, sympathising with him. 'It can be a long, slow process getting to know new people, especially in a country area like this. I have a casual arrangement whereby I often meet a group of friends in a local wine-bar on Friday evening. If you feel like coming alone…'

'Well, if you're sure you don't mind?'

'Not in the least,' Nicola assured him.

In point of fact the last thing she felt like doing was going out, but staying in moping, aching for a man she could never have, wasn't going to do her the slightest good, and besides, she reflected, it was probably time she started disabusing her friends of the notion that she was pining for Gordon.

Gordon had never really liked or approved of the wine-bar crowd, a mixed bunch of people, most of them professionals of around her own age, who liked to meet for a drink and some supper in a casual way on a Friday evening.

When Tim offered to pick her up, she was about to refuse, but then changed her mind, feeling that it might be easier if they travelled to the wine-bar together rather than for her to give him directions.

Later that evening, when she told her parents what she had arranged, her mother gave her a thoughtful look.

'I'm sorry that Matt isn't staying on. He seemed very pleasant.'

Something in her mother's voice rather than the actual words made the tiny hairs lift on Nicola's neck. Had her mother guessed how she felt about Matt? Had anyone else guessed? Had Matt himself? Was that why he had been so remote with her—so cold almost...?

Sick despair washed through her as she contemplated this possibility.

As she got ready to go out she told herself that she was glad he had gone, that now she was no longer in daily contact with him it would be much easier for her to put him right out of her mind and to concentrate on getting on with her life.

Just as she was doing right now? she asked herself grimly.

WHEN Tim arrived at eight to pick her up as they had arranged, she invited him in to meet her parents. Her mother exclaimed over his injured leg and its heavy cast.

Luckily his car was an automatic and he could still drive, he assured her, when she commented on how difficult he must be finding life.

He was easy to talk to and, although she hadn't really been looking forward to going out, Nicola discovered that she quite enjoyed the evening.

Her friends tactfully made no mention of Gordon, welcoming Tim among them, although Nicola did detect one or two raised eyebrows when she introduced him as her new boss, firmly making it clear that theirs was purely a business relationship.

Halfway through the evening Lucinda Barrett walked in without her husband and immediately made a bee-line for Nicola, greeting her as though they were long-lost friends.

Hiding her dislike of her, Nicola politely introduced her to her friends, gritting her teeth in annoyance when Lucinda smiled archly up at Tim, and commented to Nicola,

'Goodness! You haven't wasted much time in replacing Gordon, have you? Wise girl. By the way, what's happened to Matt? I haven't seen him in simply ages—although he did call round last week…'

Nicola could feel the heat crawling up under her skin, the anger she was trying hard to control making her eyes flash a little as she said flatly, 'Tim is my new boss, Lucinda, and as for Matt—he was only here on a temporary basis, but then, I expect he'll have told you that himself…'

She couldn't resist that last little jibe, suspecting that Lucinda was deliberately fabricating an intimacy between herself and Matt which had not existed—not because the other woman knew how she felt and wanted to make her jealous, Nicola knew, but because she was simply that sort of woman.

She had the satisfaction of seeing the too perfectly made-up face flush a little, a bitter look of dislike flashing from the redhead's eyes before she turned away from her and started monopolising one of the men.

'Phew! She seems rather a man-eater,' Tim commented later to Nicola when Lucinda had gone. 'Although I suppose I shouldn't say so, if she's one of your friends.'

'She's not,' Nicola assured him, adding a little uncomfortably, 'I'm sorry if you were embarrassed when she implied that you and I...well, that you were my boyfriend. I—'

'I wasn't embarrassed,' he assured her. 'Envious, perhaps...'

When she looked puzzled, he explained softly, 'You're a very, very attractive woman, Nicola, and a very intelligent one as well. That anyone should think of you as my girlfriend is a real ego-booster. I don't want to pry but I take it from Lucinda's comment that there isn't anyone special in your life at the moment…?'

Faint warning bells began to ring in Nicola's brain. She had been through this scene so many, many times before… A man—a nice, genuine, decent man—would approach her and show an interest in her, but no matter how pleasant she found him there was always that barrier of knowing that ultimately, if she allowed their relationship to grow and develop, there would come a time when she would have to tell him about her past.

Besides, she genuinely liked Tim.

'There—there isn't anyone at the moment,' she began, 'but—'

'But you don't want to get involved,' he concluded wryly for her. 'Just my luck, but this doesn't mean that we can't be friends, I hope?'

'We can be *friends*,' Nicola agreed.

'NICOLA, I haven't mentioned it to you yet, but there's a conference coming up that both of us ought to attend, according to Matt. It's being held near Bournemouth at the Grand Hotel, over the weekend of the twenty-eighth. Matt considers this conference to be very important, since it deals with various environmental issues concerning the building trade. Will you be able to come?'

Nicola nodded her head.

'It sounds interesting,' she commented. 'How long does the conference last?'

'Only a couple of days. We'll be leaving here mid-morning Friday, and we should be back Sunday evening.'

They discussed the issues likely to be raised by the conference for a few minutes before Evie appeared to say that Tim was needed in the yard.

Later that evening, when she was telling her parents about the conference, her father commented approvingly, 'A sound decision on Matthew Hunt's part, getting his business geared up in tune with the environmental issues we're all going to be confronting this coming decade. Those businesses which are first off the block in being environmentally aware are the ones which are going to be the most successful.'

That night when she went to bed Nicola wondered if Matt would be attending the conference, her body quickening with sharply painful desire.

It didn't matter how often she told herself not to do so, she couldn't seem to stop herself from thinking about him…from wanting him…from loving him.

THREE DAYS before the conference, the foreman handed in his resignation, announcing that he was going to set up in business on his own account.

After he had dealt with him, Tim turned to Nicola and commented wryly, 'I wonder how many of our men he plans to take with him.'

'If it's any comfort I doubt that any who go will stay with him for very long,' Nicola told him.

'Maybe so, but— Look, I'm going to have to

go out on site. If necessary, until we can find a replacement, I'm going to have to become an acting foreman myself.

'I've done it before. Matt came into the business the hard way himself, and he's pretty keen on all his managers at least having a basic working knowledge of the physical aspects of the building trade. Matt was a bit of a rebel when he was younger, apparently.

'He could have joined his father in the City, but instead he chose to leave school early and take off round the world. That was how he picked up his various building skills, and then, when he came back, he worked his way through university, and then decided to set up his own construction business—very small-time at first...'

A rebel... That accorded with the Matthew Hunt she remembered...the Matthew Hunt with his well-worn clothes, his casual manner, his pirate's smile, his easy insouciance after their shared night of sex.

She gave a tiny shiver. A man, given the will

to do so, could escape from the follies of his youth, and even be considered by some to be a better man for having lived through them; but a woman, even in these modern times, was still judged in a different way.

ON THE THURSDAY before the conference, Tim came into the office late in the morning and announced that he would be spending the rest of the day on one of the sites where they had run into some problems.

'Without a foreman, I really need to be there to keep an eye on what's going on. Will you be OK here? Silly question,' he continued without letting her answer. 'Of course you will. You know, in many ways you're wasted here, Nicola. You're a first-class administrator; you could become a real high-flyer if you chose…'

'I don't choose,' she told him, adding grimly, 'I've tried city life when I was younger, and I didn't like it.'

'No? Well, you aren't alone in that. Men as

well as women are beginning to wonder if they're sacrificing too much to their careers. Personally, I'm against a single-minded obsession with work.

'You're OK for tomorrow, aren't you? We're leaving here mid-morning—might as well travel there together. Pointless taking two cars…'

'Yes, my father's going to drop me off in the morning. Save me having to leave my car parked here all weekend.'

Because she wanted to clear her desk, leaving only the post to be dealt with in the morning, Nicola worked late on Thursday evening.

Tim hadn't returned to the office, and the communicating door between her office and his was closed. Several times after Evie had left she looked at it, trying not to fall into the trap of fantasising that the room beyond her own wasn't really empty at all, and that she only had to open the door to see Matt sitting at his desk working.

Once, on a ridiculous impulse, she even got up and walked across her own office, opening the door and standing there, staring hungrily at the empty desk, mentally picturing Matt's lean frame on the other side of it.

There was a huge lump in her throat, an agony of need and love that was almost a physical pain, and there was anger as well...anger against herself that she should behave so foolishly, so self-indulgently, and so potentially self-destructively.

CHAPTER EIGHT

AT EIGHT o'clock on Friday morning, Nicola's father dropped her off in the yard. She had her suitcase with her, containing all that she needed for the weekend.

The suit she was wearing wasn't new, but she felt comfortable in it, and it travelled well, even though the plain grey skirt seemed to have shrunk a little the last time it was cleaned, so that it was a little bit shorter than she would have liked.

The jacket that went with it was long and double-breasted, a fine red line breaking up the plainness of the silky lightweight woollen fabric. The suit had been expensive, but well worth the money she had paid for it, as Evie confirmed when she walked into the office an hour later and admired.

'You look great! Really brill… Pity you didn't have a bright red shirt to wear with it, though.'

Nicola hid a smile. Her plain cream silk shirt was a deliberate choice. Not for her the scarlet that Evie would plainly have preferred.

A tiny frown married her forehead. Once she had worn scarlet… A scarlet lipstick. Her hand trembled a little as she slid a piece of paper into her machine.

She had another suit in her case, and a pair of neat pleated walking shorts and a thick sweater, just in case any impromptu meetings took place in the large grounds that surrounded the hotel; in her experience there was nothing more uncomfortable than trying to walk across a smooth lawn in high-heeled shoes, and the shorts were tailored enough to reinforce her business image.

It had been her mother who had pointed out that there could well be a certain amount of formality over dinner on Saturday evening, suggesting that it might be as well for her to take a dress with her. Unwillingly she had allowed herself to be persuaded into adding her navy silk—unwillingly, because she didn't think she could ever wear it again without thinking about Matt…without remembering how he had held her and kissed her.

They had been due to leave at ten-thirty and, when Tim had not arrived at that time, Nicola checked her watch a little anxiously.

She knew that he had intended to visit a couple of the sites before they left, but she had no idea which ones and, since three of their sites were ones which couldn't be reached by phone, she was just wondering anxiously what she should do, when Evie exclaimed excitedly,

'Matt—Mr Hunt has just arrived!'

Nicola had barely managed to quell the frantic, sickening twisting in her stomach when the door opened and Matt walked in.

He was wearing a suit, a very expensive and well-tailored suit, she noticed, an immaculate half-inch of laundered white cuff protruding from its dark-clothed sleeves.

'If you've come to see Tim, I'm afraid—'

'I haven't.'

He sounded terse and irritable.

'Evie, if we could have some coffee… Nicola, if you could come through into the office, I'd like to have a word with you.'

He had remembered her. He was going to sack her. He had found out how she felt about him…

Sick with tension, Nicola followed him through into the other office, numbly noticing how he waited for her to do so and then closed the door behind her.

'I'm afraid there's been a slight accident,' he told her. 'Tim missed his footing on site yesterday. Luckily he hasn't done too much damage, but it means that, as far as he's concerned at least, the conference is out. However, that makes it even more imperative that you attend. I've discussed the whole thing with him, and we both agree that you're more than capable of judging what will and what won't be of importance to this part of the organisation…

'But no one wants to force you into something you may not feel you want to do…'

Nicola's head was whirling. Matt's anger wasn't directed at her, there was nothing personal in it at all; he was simply irritated because Tim's accident meant that Tim would not be able to attend the conference, and that both he and Matt would have to rely on her to use her judgement to ensure that she evaluated its information properly. What he was asking her was, was she prepared to take Tim's place and attend the conference without him?

'I'll have to go home and get my car,' she heard herself saying almost stupidly. 'But of course I'm quite prepared to go. I'm sorry about Tim's accident, will he—?'

'He'll be fine,' Matt told her shortly, breaking off as Evie knocked on the door to tell her to come in.

While she was handing them their coffee, he said tersely to Nicola, 'So the conference is still on, then. Good. You won't need your car, by the way. You'll be travelling with me.'

Travelling with *him*! Her hand trembled, sending coffee slopping over the sides of her mug.

If he was going to the conference, why did he need *her* to be there? Surely—?

'Of course, I'll be there in a different capacity. I'm giving a lecture on the benefits of finding alternative sources of timber, so that we can do our bit to halt the destruction of much-needed forests, although of course a good deal of progress has been made in that direction already…' He went on to talk about the importance of the conference, but Nicola could hardly take in what he was saying.

She was still trembling violently inside, so much so that she had had to put down her coffee untouched.

If she had known that attending the conference without Tim meant that she would have to travel with Matt… She swallowed hard.

'We're already running late,' she heard Matt saying. 'I don't want to rush you, Nicola, but if you're ready…'

Ready…ready? She would never be ready for this—for such unexpected and dangerous intimacy with him, for the mixture of elation and anguish which seized her every time she saw him. She needed time, time to prepare herself, to guard herself…

She was behaving like a fool, she chided herself as she saw him walking towards the door. All this fuss, all this fear and pain simply because she was going to be sharing a car journey with him. Had she really so little control over herself…over her emotions…over her love… that she really feared she couldn't sit beside him for the space of a few hours without betraying what she felt?

Totally unable to look at him, she hurried towards the door he was holding open for her.

CHAPTER NINE

THEY had been driving for just over an hour when suddenly Matt pulled off the motorway and on to a quiet side-road.

When he drove into a small village and parked the car outside an ivy-wreathed hotel, Nicola looked at him in surprise.

'You didn't drink your coffee,' he told her. 'When we arrive at the conference, we'll be going straight into a working lunch. You won't even have time to find your room, never mind unpack. The first opportunity you'll get to relax, if you're lucky, will be when you go to bed tonight, and by then your head will be so full of facts and information that you won't be able to sleep.'

'You've got a pocket memo-recorder with

you, haven't you? You'll find it helpful as an *aide mémoire*—much easier than making written notes.'

He opened his car door and got out, coming round to open her door for her. Automatically Nicola got out, scrupulously avoiding allowing their bodies to touch. A small shudder convulsed her as she misjudged her timing a little so that as he leaned forward to close the car door his hand just brushed her arm.

'Cold?'

The frowning question made her stomach muscles clench. She shook her head, still bemused by the fact that he had noticed that she had left her coffee. He couldn't surely have stopped just because of that…?

Silently she followed him into the hotel. A receptionist directed them to the coffee-lounge, which was already pleasantly busy.

A waitress found them a table by one of the windows, overlooking the street.

When the coffee came it had obviously just

been freshly made. Its rich aroma made her mouth water, and suddenly, although not even ten seconds beforehand she would have sworn that a drink was the last thing she wanted, she discovered that she was longing for the richly fragrant brew.

'Feel better now?'

She looked up from the cup to discover that Matt was watching her, his own coffee barely touched. Immediately she flushed.

'And if it's Tim you're concerned about, I don't think he's done any lasting damage.'

Her flush deepened, as Nicola acknowledged herself how little thought she had actually given to Tim or what had happened to him. She was becoming far too self-obsessed, she told herself angrily.

Matt, she noticed, still hadn't drunk his coffee, although he was insisting on her having a second cup. It wasn't until she was halfway through that it occurred to her that he really must have made this stop specifically for her benefit.

Her heart jumped fiercely inside her chest, her lungs contracting as she fought to breathe in. Nonsense, she was being ridiculous. Why on earth should it matter to Matt whether or not she had a cup of coffee?

And yet, by the time they eventually left the hotel, he still had barely drunk any of his and, even though he had brought up several points concerning the conference while she was drinking hers, they were things he could have mentioned equally easily while he was driving.

What was the matter with her? she derided herself scornfully as they walked back to the car. Was she really being stupid enough to try to convince herself that she mattered to Matt on some personal level?

How could she? She was simply one of his employees, that was all.

They had reached the car now and, without thinking, she moved towards the door, at the same time as Matt reached out to open it for her.

Just for a moment she felt the hard pressure of

his arm against her body, a sensation of shock combined with sharply painful desire stabbing through her.

She was, she discovered as she moved away from him, trembling. When she got into the car and inadvertently caught sight of her own reflection in the wing-mirror, she saw with sick despair that her eyes were huge and dark, her face far too pale. Her mouth trembled as she turned her head away from Matt, defensively letting her hair swing forward to conceal her expression from him.

She was glad when he asked her if she would mind if he played some music, relieved not to have to endure the trauma of trying to make businesslike conversation with him. Quite deliberately she kept her face averted, forcing herself to pretend an interest in the dull expanse of motorway landscape beyond the passenger window which she did not feel, and yet every so often her control broke and, without realising what she was doing, she found that she had turned her head and was watching Matt, focusing almost avidly on his face…his body…just the way his hands held the steering-wheel, and that every time she did so she was filled with such an intensity of emotion and arousal, felt so sensitive to his presence, that it was almost like being without a protective layer of skin, almost as though she had already felt his touch on every part of her body and was responding to it.

By the time they reached the conference hotel she was praying that the weekend would be just as busy as Matt had warned her it was likely to be, so that hopefully it would be impossible for her to do anything other than to concentrate on what was going on.

The intimacy of the car journey had weakened her both physically and emotionally to the point where when she eventually got out of the car she barely had the strength left to stand up.

Intent only on trying to control what she was feeling, she was totally unaware of Matt coming towards her until she felt his arm round her.

'Are you sure you're OK?' he asked her in a low voice.

Hideously conscious of how much she was trembling, not daring to look up at him in case he read the truth in her eyes, Nicola somehow managed to nod her head and mumbled untruthfully, 'It's just a bit of travel sickness. I'll be fine in a moment.'

She could see that Matt was frowning as he looked at her, and her heart sank. What on earth must he be thinking? No doubt regretting that he had ever suggested she attended this conference. She was hardly presenting an image of business-like efficiency, was she?

Her fears were confirmed when Matt hesitated and said quietly, 'Look if you're *not* feeling well—'

'I'll be fine, honestly,' she assured him, starting to walk towards the hotel's main entrance, praying that she would find the resolve from somewhere to put her own personal feelings under control and to remember why she was here.

The foyer of the hotel was thronged with people attending the conference, the heat and noise which struck her as she walked in making Nicola blink and stand back a little. She had forgotten, working in her country environment, just how overwhelming and intimidating large crowds could be.

As she hesitated, she felt Matt's hand on her arm, his presence behind her, reassuring her at the same time as it scalded her with the heat of her own physical response to him.

'Wait here,' he instructed her. 'I'll check us in and collect our room keys, and then we'd better head straight for the conference hall.'

She ought to have been the one doing that, Nicola acknowledged as she watched Matt stride over to the desk. It was almost like watching the Red Sea part, seeing the way the swarming crowd seemed to part as though by magic to let him through.

And, once he had reached the desk, busy though it was, a receptionist miraculously appeared to deal with him.

Watching the way the receptionist smiled up at him, Nicola felt her stomach knot with jealousy.

She turned her head away, telling herself that her behaviour was ridiculous, wishing with all her heart that things had not gone wrong and that she was here with Tim and not with Matt. There was, she was discovering, far more bitterness than sweetness in being with him, far more pain than pleasure.

'Your key…'

She saw Matt making his way back to her, and took the key he gave her. Behind her someone in the crowd jostled her, throwing her off balance a little. She stepped forward automatically, closing the small space between Matt and herself, tensing as she felt him reach out to steady her, his fingers closing round her upper arm, the warmth of his breath burning her skin. She saw that he was frowning as he looked beyond her.

'This place is a madhouse. Let's head for the conference room.' He looked at his watch, his hand still holding her. 'It's time we were there anyway.'

As they started to make their way through the crowd, Nicola expected Matt to release her, but he didn't, and she was burningly conscious of his hand on her arm, his presence at her side as he guided her across the crowded foyer.

As they approached the conference area proper, they were stopped and handed folders of information and name-tags, before proceeding into the large room, where waitresses were beginning to serve a buffet lunch.

Almost as soon as they were inside the room, Matt was hailed by another man. Expecting him to release her, Nicola started to move away from him, but to her astonishment he didn't let her go.

'This is Nicola Linton, one of my staff,' he introduced her to the other man, who was apparently a civil engineer.

Very quickly the two men were deep in conversation, but Nicola noticed that Matt was courteously insistent on including her in their discussion, which was mainly about how the new emphasis on environmental issues was going to affect the future of the civil engineering industry.

After that it seemed to Nicola that she barely had time to draw breath, so frantic and busy did the pace become, as Matt had predicted.

It was just gone six o'clock when the final meeting of the day eventually broke up and they were free to seek out their rooms.

'Dinner tonight will be a fairly formal affair,' Matt warned her as they waited for the lift to take them to their rooms. 'I suggest we meet in the cocktail bar beforehand, say at about seven-thirty?'

Tiredly Nicola nodded her head.

There were a hundred notes she wanted to make, a hundred things she had learnt that had relevance to her own work…things she was sure she would never be able to remember if she didn't make a note of them; and it would probably take her half an hour to shower and get changed ready for dinner.

In addition to that, the air-conditioned atmosphere of the conference centre had made her long for some proper fresh air. What she really needed was a good long walk, she reflected wistfully as the lift came and they got in.

AN HOUR LATER, when her watch beeped warningly, Nicola switched off the small tape recorder, frowning a little as she did so. If the rest of the conference centre was all hurly-burly and business, then at least her room was a haven of peace and calm. She frowned again as she looked around it. She had been rather surprised by the luxury of the room she had been given. It had obviously been very recently decorated, in soft yellows defined by much deeper blues. From her window she could see out over the grounds, the room itself was furnished with good quality reproduction furniture, and her adjoining bathroom, like the bedroom itself, had quite obviously been refurbished.

She had noticed that, although the lift had been packed, she and Matt had been the only two people getting out on their floor. They were, she suspected, occupying rooms of a far better standard than would normally have been expected of someone attending a working conference. Was this yet another indication of Matt's generosity and concern for his employees?

She moved away from the window, reluctantly acknowledging that she ought to be getting changed. A small, mirthless smile twisted her lips as she recognised how little she was looking forward to the coming evening. An evening spent in Matt's company...in the company of the man she loved. Her mouth twisted even more bitterly. In theory, perhaps, a wonderful prospect, but in reality the evening was just another business meeting as far as Matt was concerned, while for her...

She took a deep breath, her eyes blinded by a sudden rush of tears.

For her the evening would be several more hours of trauma and misery, during which she would have to fight to conceal her feelings...her misery...her love...

If only Tim hadn't had that accident. If only Matt hadn't had to take his place.

She put away the recorder and went into the bathroom, quickly turning on the shower.

Half an hour later she stood in front of her bedroom mirror studying her reflection. She was wearing the navy dress and, if her face looked a little too pale, well, that would simply bear out her earlier fib that she had been feeling car sick. Provided she managed to avoid allowing Matt to look directly into her eyes, she might just be able to get away with pretending that it was a physical disorder that was making her look so pale.

She had washed her hair and blow-dried it, and now there was nothing left for her to do but to go downstairs to the cocktail bar and meet Matt.

As she locked her bedroom door, she found herself praying that she would get through the evening without saying or doing anything to alert Matt to what was really wrong with her.

It was just after twenty-five to eight when she

walked into the crowded cocktail bar. It took her eyes several seconds to adjust to the gloom and her ears even longer to adjust to the noise.

Unaware of the interested glances she was receiving from several groups of men, she stood where she was until she could get her bearings.

When she saw how glamorously some of the other women were dressed, she was glad that her mother had warned her to pack something a little more dressy than her business suits. As she looked around the room she suddenly saw Matt. He was standing several yards away talking to a very tall, very soignée brunette. She was talking earnestly to him and, when she suddenly reached out to place her hand on his arm in emphasis of whatever she was saying, the feeling that pierced Nicola left her feeling sick and dizzy.

She hated what was happening to her, hated what she was feeling, hated the feeling of being totally out of control. The room suddenly seemed oppressively hot, she felt hemmed in, trapped, panic clawed at her. She turned away, blindingly, wanting to escape but, before she could move, she heard Matt saying her name.

She forced herself to turn her head, her lips curving into a meaningless, stiff smile, but, when she looked, Matt was on his own and the brunette seemed to have disappeared.

'What would you like to drink?' Matt asked her.

She tried to clear her head, to separate herself from the emotions churning inside her.

'Mineral water, please,' she responded tensely.

'I expect we'll be sharing a table with some of the other delegates,' she heard Matt telling her as he gave their order to a waiter. 'That's the normal format at these affairs unless you're in a large enough group to occupy a full table. It's one way of getting people to mingle. What were your impressions of this afternoon, or is it too soon for you to judge?'

Nicola took a deep breath, thankful to have something on which to focus her attention, something to distract herself from the burden of her awareness of Matt the man, rather than Matt the employer.

Once she started talking about the conference, Matt kept the ball rolling, making several succinct points about what she had learnt, and gradually she felt a little of her tension starting to slip away from her.

If it could just be like this for the rest of the weekend; if she could just force herself to focus on business instead of letting her emotions get the upper hand, she might have some chance of preserving her sanity and concealing the truth from Matt. That would be the final humiliation, if he should guess how she felt.

By the time they went into dinner she was almost beginning to relax a little, although she tensed up again when Matt put his hand beneath her elbow—a polite gesture, and one which she knew had been made to her by any number of men in the past, but none of them had had the effect on her that Matt had. She knew he must have felt the jolt of tension that went through her as he touched her. She saw the way he frowned down at her when she immediately tried to step back from him, and then realised that the crush of people heading for the dining-room made that impossible.

In fact, probably because of her lack of height, she actually discovered she was being carried forwards and almost pushed off her feet.

As she stumbled a little, Matt reached for her, pulling her into the protection of his own body. It was a protective, non-sexual gesture he would no doubt have made to any woman in the same situation, but its effect on Nicola was devastating. She literally went weak at the knees, a deep, wrenching shudder vibrating through her so that she clutched automatically at his arm for support before she realised exactly what she was doing. When she did realise, she tried to draw back, but it was too late. Matt's free arm was firmly around her, holding her so close to him that she could feel the heat of his body, and the heavy, slightly unsteady thump of his heartbeat.

When she tried to move, Matt said tersely to her, 'Let's just wait a few seconds and let the first crush get past us.'

He seemed to be murmuring the words right into her ear, the sensation of his warm breath against that delicate orifice causing such a welter of sensations inside her that she could hardly control her reaction to them. Beneath the fine silk of her dress she felt her breasts swell and lift, her nipples tightening, a corresponding tiny, pulsing ache beginning deep within her body, coupled with an overwhelming desire to let herself relax against him, to press herself even closer to him, to touch her lips to his throat, his jaw, his mouth…

She had to swallow hard on the small, anguished whimper that scaled the back of her throat. Guilt and self-disgust twisted through her stomach. She found she could hardly breathe, and knew that her pulse-rate must be wildly out of control, but she dared not move, could not move until she felt Matt step back from her slightly, relaxing the protecting guard of his arm as he told her,

'I think we can go in now.'

Not daring to look at him, she fell into step beside him, only half able to concentrate on what he was saying…something about not really understanding the crowd's eagerness to eat a meal which experience must have warned them would be adequate rather than enticing.

They were the last to arrive at their particular table, and Nicola's heart sank as she realised that she was the only woman on it.

The other men were obviously all enjoying themselves, to judge by the male laughter coming from the table as they approached it.

Even though she told herself that she was being an idiot, and an old-fashioned one at that, Nicola found that she was glad of Matt's protective bulk, as he pulled out her chair for her so that she could sit down.

The silence that followed their arrival, as the men turned to look at her, was very unnerving, but nothing prepared her for the shock she received when, as Matt sat down next to her, she heard someone drawling unpleasantly,

'Well, well, of all the coincidences. So you two are together again, are you? Permanently, or is it just another one-night stand? I seem to recollect that Nicola here excels at those…'

Jonathon…Jonathon Hendry here…and what was more he had recognised both of them! Nicola could hardly believe it. She was conscious of a return of her earlier nausea, combined with an even more intense need to escape—not just from the avid curiosity she could see in all those pairs of male eyes, not even from Jonathon, and his malice, but far, far more important, from Matt himself.

Whenever she had tortured herself with visualising the scene where she had been confronted with the past, she had never imagined anything like this…never dreamed that it would be Jonathon who would denounce her.

She was barely conscious of pushing her chair

back and standing up. Matt saying her name was a distant perception, a pin-prick of awareness in a vast sea of drowning humiliation from which she had to escape.

There were still diners straggling into the dining-room. She bumped into several of them in her haste to escape, unaware of the looks of curiosity and concern that followed her unsteady flight.

At the table she had just left Matt stood up, watching her. He was just about to follow her, when Jonathon stood up as well, apologising insincerely.

'Sorry about that, old man. Didn't realise I was putting my foot in it.'

He froze as Matt turned his head and looked at him.

'I've never liked you, Hendry. That's why I ceased doing business with your firm,' Matt told him levelly. 'I don't consider myself to be a violent man, in fact, normally I find physical violence despicable. Don't tempt me to change my mind, will you?'

The other men at the table were shuffling uncomfortably in their seats. It was quite obvious to them who would be the victor in any kind of combat between them, whether verbal, mental or physical. Matt watched as Jonathon's face turned puce. He moved swiftly from one foot to the other and started to bluster.

'It was just a joke, old man… Didn't mean anything. After all, she hardly kept it a secret that she'd spent the night with you, did she? It was obvious from the state she was in when she came to work the next day what had happened. Must say I was surprised… Quite the little prude, she made herself out to be, and then goes off with you right in the middle of my father's birthday do! Surprised to see you're still together, though. After all, a man doesn't—'

'I think you've said enough,' Matt interrupted him acidly. Then he added contemptuously, 'I'm sure you gentlemen will understand if I don't join you for dinner… I've suddenly lost my appetite.'

As he walked away from the table, he was

frowning. Nicola was that girl from all those years ago…that tiny, immature little girl who had so carelessly and so dangerously—so desperately, almost—flirted with him and then…

Strolling through the foyer, he remembered how tempted he had been by her even then, how hard he had had to fight to stop himself from mindlessly and dangerously giving in to the desire she had aroused in him, not just for his sake but for hers, too. She had still been a baby, really, for all that atrocious make-up and that wild mass of hair.

He paused, his eyes narrowing slightly as he looked back down the years. *She* had recognised him, of course, even if he had not recognised her, and to judge from her reaction to Jonathon's gibe… He looked thoughtfully across the foyer, his frown deepening as he remembered how at the time he had intended to talk to her as though she were one of his younger sisters, to warn her of the danger she was running—but he had been due to leave for the States, and then there had been the complication of the unexpected surge of desire for her.

He turned round and walked back to the reception desk. The girl behind it looked at him a little uncertainly as he made his request, but then, after a moment's consideration, she handed him what he had asked for.

UPSTAIRS in her room, Nicola was frantically packing her things into her case, with no clear idea of exactly how she was going to get home, only a burning need to escape from the scene of her appalling humiliation just as quickly as she could.

She hadn't dared look directly at Matt when Jonathon had made his dénouement, and afterwards she had felt too physically ill to do anything other than give in to her need for flight.

Now as she packed, she was still shaking, shivering, really, like a terrified animal. *Why* had she not realised that Jonathon might be at the conference? *Why* had she not known that he would recognise her—both of them?

That way she could have…

What? Refused to attend the conference? She shivered more intensely. She would rather a thousand times that Matt had recognised her himself, no matter how painful that would have been, rather than endure what had just happened, although it wasn't so much the public humiliation that had panicked her.

It was what *Matt* must be thinking…knowing now who she actually was…remembering. And he *must* have remembered. She made a small, anguished sound she didn't even hear, the sound of an animal caught in a trap.

Well, it was over now. There was no way she could continue working for Matt, no way he would want to have her working for him. Even if she hadn't made a total fool of herself by rushing out of the dining-room like that, the very fact that she was who she was…

She had no idea what she was going to tell her parents. Her mouth twisted wryly. Probably the truth. She had no resources left to conjure up some suitably convincing fiction, and anyway, she was tired of living a lie…of having to pretend…of daily, almost hourly being terrified that Matt was going to look at her and remember.

She didn't hear the pass-key turn in the lock, and her first intimation of Matt's presence was when she turned her head and saw him standing in the door, sombrely watching her.

Immediately she tensed, unable to stop the wave of hot colour that burned over her skin.

'Good, you've almost packed,' she heard him saying evenly.

She went as white as she had been red, unable to control her reaction to the pain she was suffering.

She had known what would happen, of course…had known that he wouldn't tolerate any kind of relationship between them now, either personal or professional—but still, to hear him saying it, to see the coldness in his eyes and to hear the remoteness in his voice made Nicola feel physically sick with an anguish she simply could not control.

She hadn't expected that he would do this, that he would follow her up here to watch while she left…to make *sure* that she left, she reflected.

When he'd opened the door, she had been in the act of putting the last of her things into her case, and now, as she stood there shivering, he came towards her, closing the door behind him, saying curtly.

'Is that everything?'

Numbly she nodded, biting down hard on her bottom lip to stop herself from crying.

Somehow or other she managed to deposit what she was holding in the case on the bed, but when she tried to close it she was trembling so much, felt so weak that even that simple task was beyond her.

When Matt pushed her out of the way she flinched physically from him, sick with self-disgust and the horror of what had happened.

She heard him closing the case, snapping the locks tight. When he picked it up off the bed and turned towards her, she watched him numbly, still unable to look into his face.

She could see his hand, lean, hard, the nails cut short, a working hand…a man's hand…his fingertips slightly rough. She gave a deep wrench—shudder. Once that hand…those hands had touched her…caressed her…known her more intimately than any other male hands ever had or ever would, and yet she had no memory of that intimacy, no awareness of it.

'If you're ready…'

Ready? She trembled wildly. Surely…

He was still holding her case and seemed determined to keep on doing so. Did he actually want to *physically* ensure that she left the hotel? Was that the purpose behind his presence here?

She still couldn't speak. If she did… She took a deep, gulping breath of air and nodded her head, tensing as he strode past her and opened the door.

She wanted to object, to protest that he had no need to do this, no need to add this further humiliation to what she had already suffered; but she simply could not find the strength to do so.

In the lift she stood as far away from him as

she possibly could, and yet still she was acutely aware of him—of his presence…his heat…his maleness…his power.

The hotel foyer was almost deserted. As he headed for the main exit, Matt stopped her, gesturing towards the reception desk as he said curtly.

'Wait here.'

She had no option since he still had her case. As she watched him hand in her key and say something to the receptionist, she realised that she ought to ask the girl to get her a taxi, but then, perhaps there was a taxi rank somewhere outside. Most hotels did seem to have them these days.

In Bournemouth itself she could get a train—not directly home, perhaps, but to somewhere where she could change lines and then—

As she tried to clear her muddled thoughts to make some effort to pull herself free of the shocked trauma that still gripped her, Matt came back to her.

Even now his good manners didn't fail him, she noticed miserably as he opened the door for her.

She looked tensely around, hoping to see some sign of a lurking taxi, but Matt was taking hold of her, urging her towards the car park, and it would have taken more physical energy than she possessed to resist him.

It was only when she realised that he was leading her towards his parked car that she stopped, but he seemed not to notice her shock because he walked past her and opened the door, calmly placing her case in the boot.

It was cool outside, and she shivered in her thin silk dress, her body now reacting physically to the shock she had suffered.

'You're cold,' he told her quietly. 'Get in the car.'

'Get in the car…?' Nicola stared at him, her face flooding with colour again. She knew how much he must want to be rid of her, but this was taking things to ridiculous extremes. Surely he didn't think she might actually want to stay after what had happened? Surely he must realise that, no matter how badly she had behaved in the past, she was an adult now, not a child.

'There's no need for this,' she told him huskily. 'I can get a taxi. I realise you want me to leave—'

'We're both leaving,' Matt interrupted her curtly. 'Now please get in the car.'

They were *both* leaving? Nicola's guilt increased tenfold. Confronted by Jonathon's gibe, she had thought only of herself, her own reactions, now she was forced to realise that Jonathon had not only humiliated her, but that he had also humiliated Matt, although in a different way.

Matt wasn't that casually-dressed, insouciant young man of eight years ago any more. Now he was a respected, astute businessman, whose credibility could suffer untold damage if it became public knowledge that he had attended such an important conference accompanied not so much by a responsible member of his staff, but by a woman with whom he was having some kind of brief sexual fling—which was what Jonathon had been intimating, and what Jonathon would continue to intimate, and enjoy doing so, she recognised as she shivered on the tarmac.

She wasn't aware of Matt coming towards her until she heard him say warningly, 'The car, Nicola,' and realised from the look on his face that if she didn't do so voluntarily she could quite easily find herself being placed bodily and forcibly in that vehicle.

Shakily she walked away from him and got into the car. If she had thought the drive out here an ordeal, then how on earth was she going to endure the return home?

The only thing she could do, she decided sickly when Matt got in beside her and started the engine, was to turn away from him and pretend she had gone.

That way, at least they would both be spared having to speak to one another. That she owed him an apology she knew, but she had no idea how to frame it, and besides, what good would mere words do? They couldn't wipe out what had happened.

It showed how Matt felt about the incident that he had actually left the conference because of it. That realisation added to her guilt as she turned away from him and determinedly closed her eyes, barely aware of the soft click of the central locking system being activated as Matt set the car in motion.

No matter how urgently he wanted to talk to her, he couldn't do so now…not here at the hotel…and certainly not while he was driving.

He glanced at his watch.

It was close to nine o'clock now… Which meant that it would be going on for midnight before they got back. He looked thoughtfully at Nicola's still form. She was far too tense really to be asleep. As he studied the soft sweep of her hair, so softly silky and sleek, he smiled to himself, remembering the mass of tousled curls, the too bright clothes, the startling make-up… No wonder he hadn't recognised her—at least, not visually.

His body might have done, though. It had certainly reacted to her with a startling intensity. And his emotions? He tensed a little, remembering how often he had thought about her when he was in America...how quickly he had tried to contact her once he got back. Only she had left then, and according to her former employers she had not left any forwarding address.

He thought he was beginning to understand why. He hadn't missed the way she had been watching Jonathon, that night, when she'd thought herself unobserved, and he had had enough experience of teenage girls from his own sisters to recognise one in the throes of a bad crush. Initially that had been one of the reasons he had played up to her—because he felt sorry for her, and because he hadn't particularly liked Jonathon Hendry even then.

Tense with misery, Nicola stared out of the car window, longing for the journey to be over. With any luck her parents would be in bed when she got back, which at least meant that she would not have to make any explanations to them until tomorrow. Tomorrow… She smiled painfully to herself, wishing she were a hundred years away from what was happening to her, and knowing that no matter how much time passed she would never forget the anguish of this evening.

CHAPTER TEN

'NICOLA.'

As the familiar male voice penetrated her sleep, Nicola reluctantly opened her eyes, awareness flooding back to her as she recognised the interior of Matt's car, and remembered what had happened.

The car was now stationary but, when she looked through the window, instead of the familiar outline of her parents' home, all she could see in the darkness was the shape of an irregularly built, low-roofed cottage.

As she turned towards Matt, he forestalled her questions, saying firmly, 'I think you and I need to talk, don't you?'

To talk, at this time of the night? It was almost midnight, and anyway, what was there to talk about? It went without saying that Matt would expect her to hand in her resignation, and no amount of apologising on her part could wipe out what had happened, but before she could voice these thoughts Matt was opening his car door, apparently taking her agreement for granted as he walked round to her side of the car and opened the door, waiting for her to alight...or making sure she couldn't escape, Nicola reflected shakily as she got out.

As Matt guided her towards the cottage he told her quietly, 'I thought it would be more comfortable for us both if we talked here rather than at the hotel.'

Nicola wanted to protest that she wanted to go home, but he was already inserting his key in the lock and opening the door, reaching past her to switch on the lights.

The hallway was narrow and dark, stairs leading sharply to the upper floor, doors opening to the left and right of the passage. Matt opened the right-hand one, indicating that she was to go inside.

Weakly she did so, blinking a little in the electric light as she stepped into the cottage's sitting-room.

It was simply but comfortably furnished, and more homely than she would have expected from rented premises, due in the main to the books scattered throughout the room.

'I prefer reading to watching television,' Matt informed her, startling her with the ease with which he had read her mind. 'Sit down, while I make us both a hot drink.'

Again she wanted to protest that she didn't want a drink; she felt as though she was caught up in some sort of strange waking dream, in which she herself had no control of events, and could only participate under the direction of someone else.

It was an odd, weakening sensation, and must surely have had something to do with the trauma she had experienced, but even recognising that fact did not seem to enable her to do anything about it and, even while her stunned brain formed the thought that there was nothing to stop her from getting up and walking out of the cottage, Matt reappeared carrying two mugs of coffee. She was sitting in one of the deep leather chairs either side of the fireplace and, when Matt came towards her, she flinched back from him automatically, cringing as he put down the cup of coffee—not from him, but from herself and from all that she had caused to happen.

It seemed that he stood watching her for a long time before asking quietly, 'You aren't afraid of me, are you, Nicki?'

She wasn't sure if it was the quietness of his voice, or the use or the small, personal diminutive of her name that caused her throat to lock, so that she could only shake her head in response to his question.

'I'm sorry about what happened this evening, and I'm sorry too that I didn't recognise you before.' He gave her an odd look. 'Perhaps if I'd paid more attention to my senses I might have done.'

While Nicola was still staring at him, wondering why on earth he was being so calm, so nice to her, when in reality he must be furiously angry with her and bitterly contemptuous of her into the bargain, he held out his hands to her and very gently took hold of her own.

Too bemused to resist, she allowed him to draw her to her feet, and lead her over to the settee.

'I think we'll be able to talk far more comfortably here, don't you?' he asked her steadily.

His smile disappeared as he told her.

'Hendry's comment was offensive in the extreme, and I'm not surprised that you were so upset but—'

'But it wouldn't have happened if I'd been honest with you and told you from the start who I was,' Nicola interrupted him shakily. 'Yes, I do know that. I...' She could feel tears burning her eyes, and shook her head impatiently, trying to disperse them. Breaking down in tears now was the last thing she wanted to do, but she hadn't been prepared for Matt being so kind, so understanding, so...so nice.

'Well, maybe—but in the circumstances I think I can understand why you didn't. Is *that* why you've held me so firmly at bay, Nicki…because of that night?'

The conversation wasn't following the course she had expected at all. She gave him a grave, hunted look before saying despairingly, 'Do you blame me? After—after that night with you…when I got to work and Jonathon said— when he—' Her lips were trembling so much that she had to stop speaking.

'What exactly *did* Jonathon say?' Matt pressed her, his voice suddenly hard.

She couldn't go on, and yet she had to. She owed Matt that much, at least.

'He—he made it plain that since I'd…since I'd obviously spent the night with you, I'd be quite happy to—to do the same thing with him. He also made it quite plain just how he—how all men regarded someone like me who went to bed with a man without really knowing him…who went in for one-night stands,' she told him sickly, unable to look directly at him now, but determined to spare herself nothing.

'I—I couldn't cope with it…with the gossip and innuendo, with Jonathon's comments about—about me. I handed in my notice and came home determined to make sure that no man would ever, ever again have any reason to believe that I was—that I was the sort of girl who went in for casual sex,' she went on bleakly.

'But unfortunately that kind of thing can't just be put behind you so easily. I—I was afraid that—'

She stopped, unable to go on, until Matt said gently, 'I think I understand what you're trying to say, Nicki, but you must have eventually realised, the first time you did make love, that there had never been anything physical between you and me, and that all I was doing by letting you think there had was trying to shock you into acknowledging how dangerous that kind of behaviour could be. It was obvious to me that night we met just how innocent and naïve you were, and it was equally obvious that all that determined flirting wasn't for my benefit, but for Jonathon's. I had three teenage sisters. I knew how teenage girls behave. For some reason you reminded me of them, and I couldn't help thinking how I'd feel if some man took advantage of them in the way that—

'When you fell asleep in the car without giving me your address, I decided the best thing I could do was to take you home with me and let you sleep it off. I promised myself that when you woke up in the morning you were going to get the biggest big-brother lecture you'd ever heard, but then I overslept and I had that damned plane to catch—' He broke off abruptly, suddenly aware of how pale she had become, how tense and disbelieving.

'What's wrong?' he asked her urgently. 'Nicki, what is it?'

He had to repeat the question several times before she seemed to hear it, her voice strained and low-pitched as she demanded huskily, 'What do you mean, there hadn't been anything physical between us?'

Now it was his turn to tense.

'Exactly what I said,' he told her after a brief pause. 'You and I were never lovers. Nicki, you were just a child, a drunken child at that. You surely don't think that I would have…?' He shook his head.

'And even if there was no one else before me, you and Gordon…'

He stopped when he saw her face.

'How could I?' she demanded passionately. 'How could I, after what I'd done…when for all I knew…? How could I ever explain? I would have had to have lied.' She gave a deep shudder. 'I was living a lie as it was…pretending to be something I wasn't. I didn't dare allow myself to become involved, to fall in love…to have to pretend.'

She swallowed painfully. 'You're a man. You won't understand. But after that night…after what Jonathon said to me…when he made me realise that because I'd been to bed with you and he knew it he and other men would think that I was—that I would—'

'That you would be sexually available to him,' Matt finished bitingly for her. 'Are you really trying to tell me that because of—because of *that* you've denied yourself the knowledge, the fulfilment of your own sexuality? But Nicki, Nicki, *nothing* happened! I never touched you.' He was shaking her gently, groaning under his breath as he saw the tears she couldn't hold back any longer.

'But in the morning you said… You—'

'Ah, yes. That. I didn't intend that to happen. But—well, let's just say I was as shocked as you were, but I was a lot better at concealing that shock. I tried to get in touch with you, you know,' he added, watching her. 'When I got back from the States I tried to trace you, but they told me at Mathieson and Hendry that you hadn't left any forwarding address… Was *that* why you broke up with Gordon?' he asked her quietly. 'Because he wanted—?'

Nicola shook her head, stopping him, a shaky laugh trembling through her. 'No, it was nothing like that. The last thing Gordon wanted from me was sex. No…'

'But you still love him…?'

'*Love* him?' She gave Matt a shaky look. 'I never loved him. We were just friends—barely that, really. It was convenient for us to date one another.' Her voice became slightly bitter. 'It was safe…'

'Because Gordon wouldn't ask for sex. Oh, Nicki, what have I done to you?' he asked her remorsefully. 'I had no idea…never dreamed…'

She shook her head.

'It wasn't your fault, it was mine. I should never have behaved like that in the first place, then Jonathon would never…'

She heard Matt groan and stopped speaking.

'You were a baby, that was all, just a baby.' He gave her a fierce look and added forcefully, 'And I'll tell you this, if I *had* made love to you, drunk or not you would have been able to remember it…'

Something quivered deep inside her, a soft, fluttering sensation that made her tense her body automatically, even as she drew in a tiny, shocked gasp of breath.

'I wanted to, you know,' she heard Matt saying to her. 'I think that's what made me so angry with you—the fact that even knowing you hadn't the least interest in me, despite all that determined flirting, I still wanted you. In fact, I still do...'

She stared at him, trembling inwardly.

'But you can't,' she protested. 'Not after everything that's happened. Not after tonight and Jonathon...and the conference...'

'To hell with Hendry and the conference. What's far more important right now is you and the way I feel about you. I want to make love to you, Nicki,' he told her shockingly.

'Because you feel sorry for me?' she questioned sharply, her expression defensive. 'Because you feel—'

'Because I feel such a need for you that I can't resist it...or you,' Matt corrected her, and she thought she heard him saying as he lowered his

mouth to hers—but she couldn't be sure—
'Because I love you.'

It was useless trying to tell herself to stop him;
her senses drank in the intimacy of him so greedily
that their need obliterated everything else.

She trembled as his hands slid into her hair,
tenderly holding her captive as he kissed her,
slowly, lingeringly as though he wanted to
savour each individual millisecond of pleasure,
his lips brushing hers, sensitising them, until
they clung eagerly to his, urgently seeking a
deeper pressure, a greater intimacy.

'If you don't want me, you'll tell me, won't
you?' Matt whispered between kisses.

If she *didn't* want him! It must be shamefully
obvious to him how much she *did* want him, she
reflected dizzily as she clung to him, her nails
digging into the firm flesh of his back in a sharp,
involuntary reaction to the passionate intensity
of his kiss. The top half of his body was covering
hers, pressing her back into the settee. She could
feel the unsteady race of his heartbeat, the heat

coming off his flesh. As she closed her eyes, she could visualise his body, hard and male, his skin satin-sleek over his muscles, strong and powerful. A deep shudder ran through her, but when Matt mistook the reason and started to lift himself away from her she clung to him.

Immediately he responded to her unspoken plea, wrapping her in his arms and holding her against him while he kissed her throat and caressed the narrow line of her shoulder. Her skin burned where he touched it, her clothes an unbearable barrier between them. She ached for him to touch her skin with an intensity she couldn't contain. When he stroked her lips with his tongue-tip, she made a small, taut sound deep in her throat that caused him to deepen the kiss to a level of intimacy that sent pleasure jolting through her body at the same time as it made her ache and move frantically against him.

Nicola wanted to touch him everywhere, to stroke him, to caress him, to taste him and show him… She made a soft, whimpering sound as he broke the kiss and buried his mouth in the hollow of her throat.

When his hands touched her breasts, gently holding them, shaping them, the need to be free of her clothes was so intense that she had to stop herself from crying it out loud to him. But he seemed to know what she was feeling because he reached behind her and gently lowered the zip so that he could ease the fabric away from her, telling her thickly as he did so, 'If I had made love to you then, that first time, I would have done so like this, slowly and gently, trying not to frighten you…trying to control what you were doing to me.'

He was touching her skin was he spoke, cupping her breasts, finding the hard, betraying points of her nipples and caressing them, telling her in between kisses, 'You would have felt just the way you do now—soft, feminine, your body willing to be responsive to mine. I'd have known then that you'd never known the kind of intimacy I wanted to share with you, the kind of desire that drives a man to caress a woman's body, not just with his hands but with his lips, his tongue.'

He was sliding her breasts free of the silk covering of her bra as he spoke. In the shadows of the room her flesh gleamed palely, the aureolae of her breasts darker, her nipples tautly hard peaks that seemed to beg for the intimacy he was promising.

'Then you'd have looked at me just the way you are doing now, and your body would have looked just like this, your breasts all feminine temptation, so much temptation that I wouldn't have been able to stop myself from touching them…tasting them.'

Nicola watched tensely, tiny shudders running through her as Matt slowly bent his head to her breasts, cupping them in his hands as he gently kissed them.

An aching need burst into life inside her, a sharp desire to arch her back, to catch hold of his head, to hold him there against her breast while he— Heat seemed to burst out of all her pores, a strangled sob stifled in her throat as she fought not to do what her instincts were urging her to do, but Matt seemed to sense her need because his mouth sought the aching peak of one breast, his lips caressing it gently, and then less gently when he felt her shuddering response.

The shock of the sensation engulfing her made her cry out, a high, sharp sound of shocked pleasure and need, her body arching as she offered herself to that need like a sacrifice to some pagan religion.

'Beautiful, you're so beautiful,' she heard Matt muttering against her skin, the words a litany of praise and worship as his mouth continued to feed on her aching breasts, creating a mindless sea of sensuality to surround them with warm, lapping waves of increasing arousal.

Only when her own need to reciprocate, to touch him with the same intimacy with which he was touching her, became too much for her, did Nicola push him away, struggling to explain to him when he held her and kissed her, apologising for shocking or hurting her, that what she wanted was to be able to touch him without the barrier of their clothes, to be able to see if his body reacted to her the way hers did to him.

The words were fragmented, unstructured, and uncertain, but Matt still seemed to be able to make sense of them, guiding her fingers to his shirt, helping her unfasten the buttons, groaning softly when she tried to tug his shirt off and became side-tracked into exploring the hard leanness of his chest with her lips, fascinated by the flat hardness of his nipples, wanting to know if he would react to her the way she had to him, awed to find out that he could and did, half thrilled, half shocked by the things he said to her, by the things he promised her.

At eighteen this intensity of passion would have terrified her, she suspected, but she wasn't eighteen now, and far from being terrified—

'Much more of this and there'll be no going back, you know that, don't you?' Matt warned her hoarsely as she reached for his belt.

Her eyes followed his movements, her body

shuddering with excitement as she watched him remove his clothes. He studied her gravely for a moment before holding out his arms to her, and she recognised that in doing so he was asking her to make her own decision, to choose freely of her own accord to go to him or to withdraw.

He was standing in front of the fire. Only half a dozen paces or so away but, as she got up from the settee and walked unsteadily towards him, Nicola knew they were the most difficult half a dozen steps she would ever have to take.

When she reached him and his arms folded around her, she discovered that she was trembling not just with arousal, but also with relief.

Relief that she had found the courage to come to him, relief that she was here held safely in his arms. A relief that combined with the knowledge that, no matter what else the future might hold, no matter whether Matt only wanted her fleetingly—so fleetingly that this one night might be all she had of him—she would never, ever regret what they were sharing.

He might only feel desire for her, but it was a clean, honest desire…a pure desire in its way…a desire that by its very intensity would burn itself clean of any taint.

And for her there would be no regrets, no guilt…nothing but the knowledge that he had wanted her, and that that wanting had been strong enough to make their coming together special…sacred to her, if not to him.

As Matt held her, gently removing her clothes so that they stood body to body, warmed by each other's skin, each other's passion, she felt such a deep, flooding sense of joy that she actually trembled with the force of it, instinctively lifting her face, inviting his kiss, opening her mouth to the deep penetration of his tongue, welcoming the urgent stroke of his hands against her body, his arousal, his maleness.

When he touched her his hands were gentle, knowing, leading her tenderly towards the intoxicating discovery of her own sensuality, until her response to him overwhelmed them both and he told her huskily how much he wanted her, how much he needed her.

When he lowered her to the floor, protecting her from its hardness with the cushions he had dragged off the settee, she shuddered tensely, wanting him, aching for him so much that the sensation of him moving gently against her so sensitised her already aroused flesh that she cried out to him in frantic need, causing him to forget caution and surge into her. And each powerful thrust of his body was so intensely erotic that she quickly became lost in the sensations he was arousing, clinging to him, begging him never to let the pleasure stop, crying out loud to him in awed disbelief when her body finally became caught up in the fierce spiral of completion.

The sense of fulfilment that followed the frantic, driving race of desire, when Matt held her in his arms, tenderly stroking the damp hair back off her face, kissing her eyelids and the tip of her nose, and then finally and lingeringly her mouth, made her eyes burn with unexpected tears. Tears which Matt did not seem to find strange at all as he wiped away their dampness and then kissed her moist skin. An exhaustion that was as much mental as physical suddenly washed over her. Despite her efforts not to do so, she discovered that she was closing her eyes, giving up the fight to stay awake.

Watching her, Matt touched her mouth tenderly, his heart so full of emotion that he felt his own eyes prick with tears.

All these years and she had thought…had never known… He would never be able to forgive himself for that, even while selfishly, malely, he recognised with wry acceptance, he had also felt a certain raw pleasure in knowing that he was her first lover, in knowing that the pleasure they had shared was so new to her, so natural and instinctive, so responsive to his own desire that there had been times when he had feared he might lose his self-control, and spoil things for her.

He stood up, and then slowly picked her up,

carrying her upstairs and settling her in the old-fashioned double bed that dominated his bedroom, before going back downstairs to retrieve their clothes and replace the cushions on the settee.

Then broodingly he went back upstairs. She had given herself to him with every evidence of passion and pleasure, but she had not said she loved him…had not— He himself had been surprised at the speed with which he had fallen in love with her, but knowing what he did now… Who knew? Perhaps subconsciously some part of him had recognised her, had known, and that was why he had felt so drawn to her, so quickly. Now they were lovers, but he wanted far more from her than mere physical desire—much, much more.

As he climbed into bed and lay down beside her, she turned towards him in her sleep, nestling close to him, her lips curving into a soft smile as she reached out for him. He bent his head to kiss her and realised she was not as deeply asleep as he had supposed when she sighed rapturously

beneath her breath and moved her body entic-
ingly against him.

This time the pace of their lovemaking was
different, more knowing, more shared, Nicola's
confidence in herself as a woman allowing her
to indulge her desire for an intimacy with him
that she had never previously dared imagine.

She discovered how intoxicating it was to
touch his body with her hands and with her
mouth, and to discover how intensely each caress
aroused him, and not just him… There was, as
she quickly discovered, a distinct and erotic
pleasure to be found in the knowledge that she
was arousing him—that she could make him as
vulnerable as he had made her simply by letting
her fingertips drift along his thigh, simply by
circling her tongue-tip around his nipple and
then by teasing it with delicate, cat-like laps,
which drove him into a frenzy of hoarse protests
and male pleas that she cease tormenting him.

Later, though, when her own desire incited her
into more intimate caresses, she was the one who

trembled when she felt and saw his body's response to the delicate exploration of her finger-tips and lips; but when she would have drawn away from him, half afraid of the intensity of his arousal and her own aching reaction to it, he stopped her gently, whispering to her how much pleasure she was giving him…how much he loved the way she was touching him, the intimacy of her caresses, even while the pleasure she was giving him was almost more than he could bear.

'Let me show you what it feels like,' he whispered to her. 'Let me show you how it feels to be loved so pleasurably.'

She trembled convulsively at the thought of so intimate a loving, holding her breath in a mixture of tension and delight when he touched her, half afraid of the intensity of the sensations his touch gave her, struggling to hold back the tide of arousal starting to swamp her, unsure if she wanted to commit herself to so much intimacy, so much pleasure, and yet at the same time unable to deny what was happening to her.

When she cried out at the peak of that pleasure, almost unable to endure it, Matt responded to her need, holding her, soothing her, caressing her tenderly until the spasms of sensation had faded to a blurring after-glow, before taking her and showing her that, intense though that sensation had been, there was a very special kind of pleasure and sharing that came from the intimacy of their bodies moving easily together towards a shared climax.

Afterwards, when she was on the verge of sleep, Nicola wondered what would have happened if he had loved her like that all those years ago. Her body trembled as she acknowledged how hard she would have found it to have left him in the morning—indeed, how difficult she *would* find it to leave him in the morning.

She still wasn't entirely sure why he had made love to her—if it had been out of compassion, pity, or guilt as well as the desire he had told her over and over again that he felt.

What she *did* know with an even sharper clarity than before was how much she loved him. Not just emotionally, not just sexually, but with a spiritual blending of all that was strongest and most powerful within her. Yes, she loved him, but was she strong enough to walk away from him…to be glad for what they'd had without seeking to look for something more?

When she fell asleep her eyes were wet with the tears she knew to be only the precursor of many, many more tears that were going to fall.

'NICKI, wake up.'

The voice, the hand on her arm—both of them were so instantly familiar that she was saying Matt's name even before she was properly awake, opening her eyes to discover that he was standing beside the bed, half dressed, his torso still bare and slightly damp like his hair…just as he had been eight years ago.

There was even a mug of coffee on the table beside the bed, and from the grim expression in

Matt's eyes Nicola suspected that he was probably already regretting what had happened… already—

As she turned her head away, dreading what she might read in his eyes, his hand came out sliding against her jaw, cupping her face, holding her still so that she was forced to look at him.

'Don't turn away from me,' he whispered huskily.

The emotion in his voice startled her, her glance searching his face uncertainly.

'I don't want to rush you, to force you into a commitment you aren't ready to give… But after last night you must have realised how much— how much I love you.'

Nicola stared at him, her shock showing in her eyes.

'You love me? But you *can't*. You never said… You didn't—'

'I didn't what?' he asked her softly. 'I didn't *show* you how much you mean to me, how much I love you? Do you honestly believe that—do you honestly think that if I didn't love you I would have…?'

He stopped speaking, shaking his head as he said bitingly, 'I promised myself I wouldn't do this, that I wouldn't pressurise you…that I wouldn't beg…that I'd let you— Oh, God, I'm behaving like the worst kind of fool…and worse. Nicki, I'm sorry. I never intended—I suppose it's just the strain of loving you…wanting you…of being terrified that if I let you walk out of here you'll be walking out of my life and that you'll never, ever walk back into it. I let you go once…lost you once. Maybe then I didn't know quite what I was losing, but I know now. Nicki, if you don't care…if you feel you're *never* going to be able to care, then for God's sake say so. Don't let me make an even bigger fool of myself than I already have. If you don't love me…'

She made a tiny anguished sound that checked his words and made him look at her, anxiously searching her face, hungrily absorbing the infor-mation he could see in her eyes, and then more slowly studying her again, both his hands cupping her face as he watched her, saw the love in her eyes, registered and recognised it.

'You love me?'

Nicola nodded her head, unable to speak, unable to believe this was actually happening.

'You love me…you really love me!'

He was covering her face with tiny exultant kisses as he spoke, his body trembling a little as he lowered himself on to the bed, reaching for her beneath the bedclothes, holding her against him as his mouth caressed hers, slowly, possessively, and then far more fiercely, compelling her to respond to him, to cling to him, while he told her over and over again how much he loved her.

Later, a long time later, when they had both finally come down to earth, they talked in soft-voiced murmurs, exchanging confidences, making plans, promises.

'I never meant to cause you so much pain,' Matt told her as he held Nicola in his arms. 'I feel so guilty about that…about not taking the time to reassure you before I left for New York that nothing had happened between us. I had no idea it would traumatise you so much. I only meant to give you a fright, to make you stop and think about what you were doing, about the risks you were running.'

'It wasn't your fault,' Nicola reassured him lovingly. 'If Jonathon hadn't—'

Matt put his fingers across her lips. 'Shush. He's the last person I want to talk about right now.'

'But if it hadn't been for him, this might never have happened,' Nicola pointed out teasingly.

Matt shook his head.

'Sooner or later this *would* have happened,' he told her firmly. 'Maybe not as quickly nor as intensely, but I'd started loving you long before last night. I wanted to get closer to you, but every time I tried you seemed to reject me. I thought it was because of Gordon…'

'I was afraid,' Nicola admitted. 'Afraid of responding to you because of what had happened, because I felt so guilty…so ashamed.'

Matt turned her round in his arms, cupping her face as he told her seriously, 'Even if we had made love that night, even if that night—or any night—had happened with someone else, it wouldn't make any difference to the way I feel about you. You were a child, Nicola, that was all—barely aware of what you were doing, what you were inviting… I knew that all you wanted to do was to make Jonathon jealous.'

'Not entirely,' Nicola told him, flushing slightly. 'That was what I *originally* wanted to do, but when you were dancing with me…' She stopped and looked up at him. 'I wanted you then, Matt, and I think it was knowing that I wanted you that helped to convince me that we *had* been lovers. I think that deep down somewhere I *wanted* us to have been lovers.'

When he kissed her she wrapped her arms around him, holding on to him tightly, trembling a little when he told her how much he loved her, how much he wanted her not just for now but for the rest of their lives.

'I've waited a long time to find you,' he told her lovingly. 'And now that I have found you, I don't want to wait any longer. Will you marry me, Nicki?'

When she nodded her head, he kissed her again, and this time it was she who initiated their lovemaking, touching him with loving, knowing hands, exulting in his response to her.

'WELL, NOW, Mrs Hunt, I think we should drink a toast to the person who made all this possible, don't you?'

Less than an hour ago they had arrived at their honeymoon villa on the small French Caribbean island. Outside the sun was setting in a ball of orange fire. Inside the villa the air conditioning hummed. The girl who had greeted them on their arrival, explaining that there was a meal for them in the fridge, had gone, and they were on their own.

As she took the glass of champagne Matt was handing her, Nicola laughed teasingly at him.

'Jonathon,' she guessed, giving him a deliberately provocative little pout.

'Jonathon,' Matt agreed with a grin, putting down his glass and holding out his arms to her, telling her, 'It goes dark very early here, doesn't it…?'

'Very,' Nicola agreed, straight-faced. 'In fact, it's so dark already, it might almost be bedtime…'

'You took the words right out of my mouth,' Matt told her, nibbling on her earlobe.

'But what about our supper?' Nicola pretended to protest as he picked her up.

'Later,' Matt told her. 'Much, much later. Right now I've got far more important things on my mind than food.'

'Much more important,' Nicola agreed softly. 'Much, much more important.'